I0685458

This
Route Out

Dedicated to those for
whom it is too late.

Immediately Jesus reached out his hand and caught him. "You of little faith," he said, "why did you doubt?"

Matthew 14:31

Part One
Madison

Dear Todd,

I don't really know how to do this. Dr. Woods said it would be difficult at first, but this is my third attempt at writing to you. I can't bear to start over again, so this one will have to do.

Why aren't you here, Todd? Talking to you was so much easier than this. A lot of things were.

At our session on Friday, Dr. Woods said that I should start by writing an account of what happened that night, the way I remember it. This way, if I ever doubt myself or start to feel guilty, I can look back and use this letter as a reminder that

3

I was not at fault that night. The problem is, I don't know if I was. Madison says I can't blame myself for what you did.

You said you wanted to meet me at the bonfire. I got there a little late since I was babysitting for the Robinsons two blocks over. You waited for me at our spot on the dark green bench at the bottom of the stairs to the boardwalk, nestled beside a thick overgrowth of sand reeds. Your face was cold when I got there, and at first I thought you were mad because I was late. But you never got upset over little things like that.

We went up the boardwalk and crossed onto

4

the beach. By then it had already started, our

friends from school were dancing around the flames

with cans of soda and iced tea in their hands, their

hips moving to the beat of somebody's stereo. We

exchanged hello's with a few friends before you

walked me toward the shoreline. This usually meant

we were going to sit down with our toes in the sand

while you pointed to the sky and told me about some

star or constellation I'd never heard of. You loved

the stars.

But you hadn't been yourself lately, and I

knew it. And when you sat facing me, the fire

glowing wildly in the distance behind you so that

5

you appeared to wear it as a blazing crown atop

your shaggy brown hair, I knew what was coming.

Or at least half of it. The moon shined so dimly that

night from behind a sheet of wispy gray clouds, it

was as though it wished to hide its all-seeing eyes

from the happenings of the world beneath its light.

You wouldn't tell me who she was. "It

doesn't matter." you said. "The point is that I

betrayed you, Faith. I don't deserve you." I spent

that night hiding beneath my covers, quaking as I

sobbed to the beat of every breakup song I'd ever

heard. Sometimes I wonder which track I was on

when you hung yourself in your bedroom closet.

6

We got the call at eight in the morning. It was Madison. She had seen the blinking red and blue lights of the cop cars and ambulances in front of your house on her way to work at her mom's clock shop. It was two more hours before anyone knew what had happened to you.

~Faith

Chapter One

Words. All scribbled down on a lined piece of paper. A wrinkled, torn, folded and refolded piece of paper. The edges of the paper curled in a little, the lines were faded and nearly invisible. But the words remained, dark and strong on the tattered page. The words remained, reminding me that they were invincible and that someday I would lose to them.

I folded the paper into a small rectangle and stuffed it back into the pocket of my jeans, sniffling a little while a robotic-sounding voice began announcing the stops on the intercom above my head. *Next stop, Eatonville. Estimated arrival: 9:37 pm. And after that, The Grove. Estimated arrival: 9:58 pm. Thank you for riding NJ Transit.* I unzipped the duffel bag on the seat beside me and rummaged through it for a few moments in search of my sweatshirt, which had been hiding at the bottom. I pulled it on over my head and zipped the bag back up, then rested my elbow on the sill of the large window beside me, leaning my head on the glass. The world ran backwards outside, trekking in the direction where it all began.

The Grove was one of the wealthiest towns

on the Jersey Shore. Growing up there, I had never really taken much notice of this. Your world doesn't look the slightest bit unique until you have seen another, and until I moved to New York City, mine was just another town.

It had been two years since I'd seen The Grove.

Two years since I'd tasted the moist, salty air.

Two years since I'd spoken to Faith.

I leaned away from the window to get a look at my reflection in it. My dirty blonde hair was pulled up into a sloppy ponytail with strands dangling off the sides. I pushed a couple of the strands behind my ear and smiled lightly at the face that looked back, making an attempt to convince myself that I didn't look *that* bad. A pointless effort, of course. My forehead had broken out and was painted with three or flour little red blotches of acne, faults that I had tried relentlessly to cover with concealing makeup before being driven to the train station. My lips hadn't been glossed and were thus pale. I reached into the front pocket of the bag on the seat beside me and pulled out a watermelon lip balm, then smoothed the sticky surface of the balm over my dry lips. There were still the tear streaks in

11

my makeup that ran across my cheeks, but not much could be done of them.

I sat back in the soft gray seat and stared out the window, slowly falling into step with backwards footprints. Remembering a time that could no longer be held captive beneath my thoughts.

I could still hear her crying, sometimes.

Victoria Maguire wasn't one to cry, but it seems that's all she did after the incident with Todd. He was her only son, the brother to her nine-month-old girl and the living memory of her first husband, who had died of leukemia when Todd was seven years old. He was my best friend as well as Faith's, until the day he became more than a friend to Faith and less of a friend to me.

The memory of that night had been painted over and left to rot in my mind until the day my mom called and told me about Faith.

"Maddie?"

The lull in conversation was beginning to draw attention to my own silence. I took a breath and ran my eyes over the multiple papers scattered across my desk before I began to speak again.

"How long has she been in?" I asked.

The sky outside my window was a faded

blue, painted in dustings of pink and orange clouds. The colors reflected off the innumerable windows of the buildings and skyscrapers that could be seen from the apartment, recreating the picture-perfect evening expected by the thousands of travelers who chose to temporarily inhabit the city every day.

"Two days now. Mrs. Anderson called me up from the hospital last night to ask if I could put in a prayer request in church this morning. I did; anonymously, of course. You know how these things spread."

I ran my index finger over the dull eraser of the pencil in front of me.

14

"Yeah. I know."

"I think it would really help, Madison. I'm not asking you to leave school, I know how important it is that you're there for your last week. But if you could come, maybe a week or two after graduation..."

I bit down hard on the inside of my cheek, releasing only after I realized that it was beginning to throb slightly.

"You know I wouldn't ask if it wasn't important."

I nodded as though she could see me, the motion of my head giving a final push to the drops

15

moisture welled up within my eyelids.

"Yeah," I finally managed, "yeah, I know."

As I leaned into the seat's material I could feel every last event of that night diving within my mind and shattering so that each piece surrounded me with reminders of my every mistake.

There was hardly enough light lining the streets and sidewalks to allow me to see much of the world outside, but I knew The Grove was coming closer. I could feel it.

Dear Todd,

It's been almost a week since I last wrote
you. I think it was guilt that kept me from sitting
down to do it until now.

I couldn't go, Todd. With all your family and
friends; all the people who knew you and loved you
because the two inevitably coexisted. I almost did.
Mom and Dad and Scott all went together. I told
them I was getting a ride from Madison. My real
plan was to ride my bike down to the church and
give myself time to clear my head. By the time I was
there, everyone was filing in, their black attire

17

clashing with the clean white of the church. I

couldn't do it, Todd. I left my bike on the rack next

to the side entrance and walked toward the small

cluster of trees beside the church.

Do you remember that week we worked on

the labyrinth?

That was where I went, to the clearing in the

middle of the small wood where the smooth stone

maze was laid out on the ground as it had been for

three years, since its construction was first

suggested by an elderly woman in the adult choir.

The purpose of the labyrinth was to remember one's

center; a large stone that came out of the middle

18

ground on which was inscribed a long, thin cross. It was customary to walk the maze and come to the center. Instead, I quickly crossed over the stones and sat beside the largest in the middle. It was there that I first cried for you, Todd. The numbness dissipated from my being and left room for sorrow.

Gone. How could you be gone? Why did you go, Todd? Why did you leave? You could have held out. You could have stayed strong. What kept you from staying strong? What kept you from being the guy we all thought you were? Everything's different without you. Nobody asked you to leave. How could you, Todd? How could you? You never

19

asked me for help. I was there, Todd. I could have

helped. I was there for you. I was there.

Your funeral was two hours long. I took a

seat in the shrubbery beside the steps of the church

and listened as they spoke of you. "Too soon" rang

the words reborn in the mouths of nearly every

speaker. "Too soon", "so tragic", "greatly

missed". Did you listen, Todd?

~Faith

Chapter Two

"Madison."

I swiveled around on the balls of my feet and faced a small, thin woman in a long white skirt and a turquoise tank top. From her neck hung a colorful assortment of beaded necklaces, all varying in size and shape. Her lengthy blonde hair was tied in a loose ponytail, on top of which sat a pair of large brown sunglasses. Her skin was a light tan, already sun-kissed in the early days of Summer.

"Mom," I smiled, setting down my bags on the concrete floor of the train station.

After I moved in with my dad the Summer
after my sophomore year, Mom and I had slowly
become much less connected than we had ever
been. Practically hourly phone calls and weekly
visits had slowly turned into much less predictable
and frequent contact. If it weren't for Faith, it's hard
to say what would have become of the relationship I
had with my mom. It's hard to say what would have
become of a lot of things.

Mom wrapped her arms around me and
pulled me into her tight embrace, pressing her
warm cheek to my hair. I closed my eyes and
breathed in the air, which was far fresher than that

which I had become accustomed to.

"You're home," she whispered, pulling away and resting her palms on my shoulders. "I am so glad you're finally home."

"Me too," I said, pulling down the sleeve of my sweatshirt and resting it on my palm.

She smiled and bent down to pick up the blue and white duffel beside my feet. I cooperated and wrapped my hand around the handle of my red luggage bag.

"All that's left is the kitchen sink, right?" Mom mused as she lifted the bag from the ground.

I shrugged. "Had to leave *something* for

Dad."

We stepped down off the platform and headed toward her car, the same silver Corvette convertible she had been driving two years prior to my return. In my mind's eye I could still see the way she stood beside it as the train began to move on the day I left, hands in the pockets of her blue jeans, eyes moist.

After my bags were stuffed into the trunk, I took a seat on the passenger's side and slumped down a little in the leather interior.

"You don't want to drive?" Mom asked, poking her head in the window across from me.

24

"Not really." I smiled, closing my eyes and feigning a snore.

She laughed as she opened the door, then sat down and sighed. I opened one eye and looked to see that she was staring at me, her expression wistful.

"What?" I said.

"I just love seeing you like this. You seem so much...happier. I thought I'd never see that smile again after what happened."

Pang. The subject. I had not once imagined what it would be like to hear other people bring it up before my return to The Grove. I bit my lip and waited for her to speak again, which she didn't

seem to mind. Or notice, for that matter.

"Are you excited for NYU? I cannot *tell* you

how many people ask about you, Maddie.

Especially your old teachers! They're always

wondering how school is going, always asking to

see pictures from your graduation. I just love to tell

them all about it, especially about how highly your

principal spoke of your academics to me after the

ceremony. I never have been able to show them the

pictures, of course."

I nodded. "I thought Dad sent you the

pictures? He said he was going to."

She shrugged. "You know your father."

Mom and Dad had been divorced since I was six years old after Dad was offered a job at a major law firm in the city. The suggestion that we uproot ourselves from the town my mom had grown up in was just the breaking point the relationship had been waiting for, as Mom's outgoing personality and enthusiastic spirit often conflicted largely with Dad's lack of both qualities and made for incessant arguments I could vaguely remember from my young childhood.

The car pulled out of the parking lot. Mom continued to go on about how she couldn't believe I was already a few months away from going to college, starting my adult life, etcetera. Even the circumstances of my visit could not keep her from expressing her excitement over my return.

I ran my eyes over the collection of stores on the other side of the street we rode down. *Milo's Shoe Loft*, where prices kept bennies out and designer labels kept locals swarming in. *Tito's Pizzeria,* undeniably the best place to eat in town. *Let's Ride!,* souvenir shop. Bennies only. Beside those three were a few that had been added in the time I was away, and I figured that they would probably be replaced before long. They came and went, the bakeries and dress shops that often took residence in those spots, but the three beside them, the classics, were there to stay.

"Are you hungry?" Mom asked as I eyed the inside of *Tito's*, where the boy behind the counter was tossing up a thick round circle of dough in the air for the entertainment of the girls placing their orders, who were smiling and laughing.

"What?" I stirred from contemplation and shook my head. "No, I'm fine."

We rolled by the Patterson's house, a yellow four-story home with a wrap-around porch on the ground level and a miniature one on the top floor, which was entered through a set of French doors and looked out just above the roofs of houses that lined the path to the beach.

"If you do get hungry, Mrs. Emerson brought over some lemon bars that you absolutely *must* try."

Out my window I caught a glimpse of the Wesley family's home, one of the smaller houses in The Grove, a three-story with a yard that did not extend more than a few feet from the sides of the house but had a fair sum of space from the porch to the sidewalk.

After a few other houses passed, the car

slowed and turned into the driveway of a four-story

home on the corner of Abbott Street and Ocean

Avenue. It was pale blue with white shutters. The

garage, which the car slowly rolled into, faced the

house across the street. The front door was around

the other side, where it faced Ocean Avenue, lined

by the boardwalk and the beach. Home.

Dear Todd,

I never wanted to tell you my problems. You just seemed so delicate sometimes, as if the weight of burden rested solely on your shoulders. As if telling you how I felt would only add layers to your worries.

You weren't always like that. I remember laughing with you until my stomach was in knots and your cheeks were painted red. I remember the little moments, the things I always swore I'd tell our

32

grandchildren someday. Not that I ever would have

said so to you. You never seemed all that interested

in the future, anyway. There was this one day in the

fall before you left when you asked me to come

pumpkin picking with you on that farm just outside

Redwood, the one your uncle used to work on. It

was a few days before my birthday, so you brought

along a little box of candles and used a pocket knife

to dig out indentations in the under-grown pumpkin

we'd bought. Then you took the candles and stuck

them in the pumpkin one by one until there stood

sixteen. You forgot to bring matches. "We can

imagine they're lit." you said. I took a large,

33

exaggerated breath and blew out our faux flames,

bursting out in laughter as I pretended to struggle

with the last few. When I looked back up, your eyes

were fixed on me, your expression pensive. "Did I

miss one?" I asked, still smiling. "Just one." you

said, smiling back. "But I don't think it's ever going

out."

You came in and out of being happy like

that. One week you'd hardly speak, the next you'd

wear a smile wide enough to touch both ends of the

horizon. They've tried to tell me you were putting

on an act for the people around you, but I don't

know about that. If you were pretending, it wasn't

only to convince others that you were okay.

~Faith

Chapter Three

The first thing I saw was the calendar. Beneath a picture of two golden retriever puppies running beside each other on a sandy beach was the word *June*. I walked toward the space where it hung above my dresser and ran my finger over the word before setting down my bag, turning around, and becoming once again accustomed to my old room.

The walls were a pale blue and on top of them sat multiple white picture frames, each carefully spaced so that they would not look crowded; a trick Mom had taught me after the room

36

was repainted in the beginning of my freshman year. In the middle of the room was my bed, a queen-size with a shear white canopy and at least a dozen white and blue pillows, one of which had a tan starfish embroidered on the front. This particular pillow sat in front of the others, face out, as though it was gazing out the doors across from it. I walked over to the white French doors and grasped the shiny brass handle on the right, which was cold and free of fingerprints, as it had probably been left untouched for a while. Who would have touched it, anyway? Mom never liked the balcony outside the doors, she always said it was too high up and made her uncomfortable. It wasn't like her to be afraid of anything, but of that she was. I opened the door and stepped out on the balcony.

"Did you really?" a voice sounded from below. It was followed by a plethora of giggles. The lights lining our walkway in the front yard were on, as were the old, English-style streetlights across the road by the boardwalk, thus making it easy to see below. I wrapped my fingers around the balcony railing and looked down to see a cluster of about seven or eight girls on beach cruisers slowly pedaling along the road. I considered turning on the light above the balcony and decided against it in order to keep from being seen by anyone in town before it was totally necessary. The girl in the front turned to face the others and stopped short.

"Crap!" Another girl squealed as her tire collided with that of the front girl's bike. The rest of them laughed as they hit their brakes.

"Heather, do you think I would lie about this?" the front girl said, hardly noticing the collision. Her dark brown hair cascaded over her shoulders, which were near bare beneath the thin spaghetti straps of a yellow tank top.

"You lied about kissing Marcus Gunthry just last week!" a girl in board shorts and an orange peasant top chimed in.

"Guys, shut *up*! You realize we're, like, *right* next to that house, right? If my mom gets another complaint, I'm going to be stuck watching reruns of *Full House* in my room until I'm forty." hissed a girl in the back.

"You're not going to get grounded, Sam. That's Maddie Baker's mom's house." I blushed at the sound of my name. "She's chill."

The girl in the board shorts flipped over her head and shook out her hair, then bound it into a loose pony-tail. "I heard she was coming back this Summer."

"Who, Maddie?" the lead girl asked.

"Yeah, I heard that too." one of the quieter girls said. "My mom is, like, best friends with Miss Baker. She told me Maddie was coming back to be with Faith after what happened."

I realized then that the girl speaking was Eloise Newman, Annabelle Newman's daughter. Annabelle and my mom had been friends ever since the Newman family moved to The Grove when I was in eighth grade. Mom had eventually hired her to work as co-manager of her designer clock boutique, *Timeless*, and I could vividly recollect the two of them spending countless hours at work

41

discussing new ideas for the shop and exchanging childhood memories. Eloise was only a fifth-grader when our moms met, so she and I never became very close.

"She's a little late. Faith has been out of the hospital for, like, two weeks now."

One of the girls toward the front of the pack rolled her eyes. "The whole thing with Todd Maguire wouldn't even have happened if it weren't for Faith."

I held a hand to my gut and took a deep breath. That name. How long had it been since I'd heard someone say it out loud? The comment about

Faith was to be expected, it wasn't like I hadn't heard the same in different forms countless times before from people who believed the incident was Faith's fault. But when I still lived in The Grove in the weeks before I made the move to the city, his name was never said by anyone.

The girls all nodded, except Eloise.

"Faith said Todd broke up with her that night before...you know." Eloise said rather softly. Two of the girls in front of her looked toward each other and rolled their eyes.

"If you believe what she says." one of them responded without looking back at her. "How do you know she's not crazy?"

There was a lull in the conversation while the others waited for Eloise to reply.

"It must be hard for Madison." she said, veering off subject. "I mean, I don't think she has even been back to The Grove since the Todd Maguire thing like, two years ago."

"Oh. My. God. Guys, did you see that?" one of the girls interrupted. "That was *definitely* Dylan's car that just turned around the corner!"

"He's probably on his way to the party at Aaron Wilding's house!"

"Hey, Taylor, if you're so close to Dylan,

why don't we just go over there and watch you talk to him?"

"Shut *up*, Heather! Everything I said was one *thousand* percent true!"

"Then you shouldn't have a problem!"

The group slowly began to pedal again. I watched Eloise move along with her head turned toward the shore while the others continued to cackle and gossip.

*   *   *

Back in my room, I carefully unzipped my

45

duffel bag, which snagged on multiple bulging

articles of clothing before finally opening. Inside

the bag, my clothes had been sloppily folded and

stacked on top of one another. On top of the middle

pile was a little paper note, and I recognized the

chicken-scratch handwriting immediately.

Maddie,

Hope you have a great time back

in Jersey. I'll miss you. See you soon!

Love,

Dad

The note was folded under at the bottom. I lifted it up and found two hundred dollar bills tucked inside. I remembered refusing to accept any money he offered back in New York. *"I've got plenty, Dad. I really don't need it."* I should have known he wouldn't give up that easily. That's who he was. If he didn't feel like he was meeting his obligations as a father, what with the round-the-clock shifts spent at his law firm and the many nights I was left with a drawer full of takeout menus, he would try to make up for it through bribes.

As I pulled out my clothes and began to tuck

them away in the drawers of my dresser, I examined the pictures hung up on the wall. The first one to catch my eye was one of three young children, about four or five years old, standing together. The two on either side were girls, who held dripping ice cream cones in their delicate little fingers. The girl on the left sported uneven pigtails, while the girl on the right had her hair falling over her bony shoulders. Their smiles were painted in chocolate and vanilla. Between them was a boy.

The boy's arms were wrapped around the shoulders of the girls, with his hands shaped into two thumbs up. His shaggy blonde hair covered his blue eyes a little, and the rims of his mouth were glazed with strawberry residue. His smile shined with effortless intensity.

"I can get a pack of hangers from downstairs so you can put some of your clothes in the closet." Mom's voice sounded from the doorway.

I swiveled around on the balls of my feet and faced her where she stood holding a large pile of used towels.

"It's only two weeks, Mom."

She nodded, looking rather disappointed by the news that I had yet to change my mind about the length of my visit.

49

"I know that." she replied somewhat defensively.

I walked toward her and removed a few of the towels from the pile in her arms.

"Thanks, sweetie." she said softly.

We walked across the hall to the stairs and made our way down. I looked around the foyer at the bottom, scanning the entities that had been placed in it in the time I was away. A new ovular, floral print rug laid in the middle of the wood floor and I could remember Mom telling me about it over the phone when she had bought it a few months before my return. She had raved about the young

Frenchman who sold it to her, a man she even went on to date for a few weeks before she grew bored with him.

"I talked to Tara Anderson on the phone earlier." Mom said as we stepped down onto the first floor and made our way through the Victorian-style dining room and the spacious, Tuscan-style kitchen. Mom wasn't one to be awfully decisive when it came to themes.

"How is she?" I asked.

"Better," she replied, "especially since Faith has been back home."

I nodded. "Why did they let Faith out? I

figured she'd still be there by the time I got here,

since you never said anything about her being

discharged…"

"I was afraid you wouldn't come if I told

you, Maddie. Faith started eating again. She's still

on suicide watch, though. I was afraid you'd think

she was better and that there was no need for you to

come."

We went into the laundry room and dropped

the towels in the washer. There was a little note

taped up above it where a scribbled set of directions

to clothes washing had been posted. The bottom of

the note read, "I'll see you soon, love. Don't forget

to keep the whites and colors separate this time! ~Marcella". Marcella was the maid, who usually took two or three weeks off in the Summer to visit her family in Jamaica.

"I still would have come." I said softly.

"Anyway," Mom continued, "Tara will be over in the morning to talk to you. If you're feeling up to it, maybe you could go see Faith."

My stomach jumped. I hadn't given much thought to what it would be like to see Faith again. I hadn't given any thought to what I would say. I reached for my pocket and felt inside for the folded paper, sighing lightly as my fingers ran across the soft edge of it.

Letter #5

Dear Todd,

Madison told me she was leaving today. She's going to spend a couple weeks with her dad, up in the city. I wish she wouldn't. Sometimes it seems like she's the only one who believes that everything happened the way I told it that night.

Mom took me to church yesterday. It was the first time I'd seen everyone since you left. I swear I could feel them staring at me. I know they think it was my fault. I even know they think I broke up with you, because that makes more sense than the truth.

55

Madison says they want someone to blame. It's

going to be hard feeling all of them judge me and

make assumptions while she's gone, but it's only a

couple weeks, anyway.

It feels so strange telling you what's going

on here. Honestly, I don't think you want to know.

Dr. Woods was relocated to an office up north and

my new therapist hasn't suggested anything like

this, so I guess I don't really have to do it anymore.

I don't know.

~Faith

Chapter Four

The sunlight tore through my eyelids. I sat up and glanced at the floor, where my Dragonflies logo sweatshirt was lying face down. I grasped it and pulled it on, then hopped out of bed and made my way downstairs.

The smell of bacon drifted outside the kitchen, where I could hear Mom talking softly. I walked through the foyer, passing the living area to the right and made a left through the doorway into the kitchen. I stepped down onto the cold tile floor in my bare feet.

"Good morning, sweetie," Mom said from the table, where she was sitting in a pair of tan running sweats across from a brown-haired woman in a pale pink blouse and black pencil skirt. The woman turned her head toward me and watched me walk toward the two of them through a large pair of sunglasses. After my first few steps toward the table she bowed her head slightly and lifted the glasses from her face, gently placing them atop her head. She then looked back up at me, revealing a pair of slightly puffy eyes lined with bags.

"Miss Anderson," I said, recognizing her as I slowly took a seat beside Mom at the table.

"Hi, Maddie," she replied with a weak smile.

Tara Anderson's dyed blonde hair was pulled back into a tight pony-tail. Her face hid beneath a great some of makeup, with a foundation slightly darker than her natural coloring as revealed by her neck and arms, which were pale. Across her cheeks ran lines of that pale skin, trails left behind by tears, some of which still continued their journey down to her chin. Mom reached across the table and handed her a napkin to dab at her face.

"I hate to be here so soon, I know you just got back, but…" Miss Anderson trailed off, her gaze shifting to the window beside the table occasionally, out of which could be seen the backyard. I looked in the same direction for a moment myself, catching the eye of a bird wandering around the edge of the pool. It stared inside for a moment, then hopped off the ground and flew a short distance in the other direction until perching itself on the tall white fence separating us from the Weldon residence.

"Don't worry about it, Tara. We understand." Mom responded for me.

Miss Anderson smiled back faintly and turned her attention back on me. "I know you probably wanted to get your rest, since you just got here and all."

"No, it's okay. I'm fine."

Mom stood up and pushed in her chair. "I'll be upstairs if you need me," she said, bending down to kiss my forehead before she stepped around the island and out of the room.

"How is she?" I asked after a few moments. The clock on the stove read eight a.m., and I wondered how I had been able to wake up so early after lying awake in bed for so long the night before.

Tara Anderson took a sip from the coffee Mom

must have brewed her, then gently set down the mug on the table. "I've never seen her this bad before."

"They let her out of the hospital, though," I said, gnawing at the inside of my cheek.

"She started eating again." she explained. "A week after being admitted, she looked better than I'd seen her in a long time. The color returned to her cheeks, she smiled every so often. After two weeks, the doctor suggested that I take her home and keep a close eye on her, in case she began to regress. I thought about keeping her there for a little longer, but I just couldn't bring myself to do it. She seemed so much better."

"Has she stopped eating since then?" I asked. Out of the corner of my eye I saw the belly of a lady bug moving across the outside of the window as the little insect ventured up. It slipped every so often, its little wings ejecting from its back when it did. It kept moving, though, inching toward an unknown destination.

"No." Tara replied. "It's not that. Faith never leaves, Madison. She spends entire days in her bedroom, reading or watching television. Her friends haven't called the house phone in ages, and her cell phone is never on. Sometimes I have to tell her to dress herself in the morning, otherwise she'll just sit around in her pajamas all day."

I tucked a lock of hair behind my ear and pushed the rest behind my back. "I wish I knew how to help, Miss Anderson, but…"

"Maddie," she said, reaching across the table to take hold of my hands. She grasped them firmly and looked into my eyes. "You are already helping by being here. Leaving behind your life in the city for an entire summer, it means so much to her, and to me."

I smiled weakly.

"It would be wonderful if you could take her

out a couple times while you're here, if you don't mind. Let her test the waters, get back on her legs, you know? She won't go anywhere that poses the risk of seeing someone she knows, especially someone from school. Her psychiatrist told me it has something to do with an anxiety she developed from having hid away for so long. But you could always go a couple towns over. I'd have no problem paying for gas, if that's an issue."

I began to say something, but decided against it and let her continue.

"It's like she has been asleep ever since the incident, trailing along slowly through the days and months until they turn into years. Never living, only

pretending to." Tara Anderson said softly. "I just

hoped you might help us wake her up."

Dear Todd,

I can go for stretches of hours without thinking about you now. It's funny, you were in my life for so long, but now it feels like your existence was no more than a sweet dream with a devilish twist.

When can I wake up, Todd? When can I go back to changing and moving and growing and living the way everyone else does? Your name has been erased from the headlines. Your face is no longer present on the nine o' clock news. They're forgetting. They're moving forward. Maybe this is

my punishment for being so hard on you that night.

Maybe God is trying to tell me that I wronged you,

that I've earned this suffering. It's becoming

difficult to question that I have.

I screamed at you that night. I cut your ears

with words of a quality so harsh that one might

doubt they could be conjured in the presence of a

generally good-natured mind and heart. I asked you

how you could do this to me, how you could betray

me. Were you at the edge when these inquiries

surpassed my lips?

Did I push you over?

~Faith

Chapter Five

I climbed into the back seat of the car and pulled on my seatbelt while Mom and Miss Anderson got themselves situated in the front. As we pulled out of the garage, little droplets of water began to hit the windows. I stuffed my hand in the pocket of my jeans and felt the folded paper inside, sighing.

"Faith isn't home alone, is she?" Mom asked, sounding slightly nervous.

"No, Scott's with her." Tara Anderson replied, unzipping her purse and pulling out a slim silver cell phone. She punched down on the buttons and held it to her ear. "Brad, I'm going to be a few minutes late. If the Coopers arrive before I get there, offer them a cup of coffee and tell them I'm taking a call and will be with them shortly. I'll just come in the back door. Okay, I've got to go, I'll see you soon."

Miss Anderson owned the most popular real estate agency on the shore, set in a Victorian-style home on the west side of The Grove.

We rode a few blocks down Ocean Avenue until coming to a fork in the road. The direction on the left was a road that went on for a long while along the boardwalk. I wondered if I had ever come to the end of it, but couldn't recall ever having done so. It just veered on, a path that seemed to lead beyond the horizon. We turned onto the street on the right, Brielle Lane, which led to the Anderson residence.

"Are you going to need me to pick you up from work later, Tara?" Mom asked.

"No, Brad will be picking my car up from the shop this afternoon. Thank you, though."

Mom nodded. "And you'll call me when you need a ride home, sweetie?"

"I think I'll just walk." I responded.

72

"Not if it keeps raining." she said, turning to pull into the driveway of a light gray house with stark white shutters. "Just give me a call, okay?" I nodded.

"Scott knows you're coming, he'll let you in." Miss Anderson said. "And Madison?"

"Yeah?"

"Thank you." She looked back at me when she said it, compact mirror in hand as she began the attempt to cover up the tear streaks on her face. I smiled a little and opened the door, stepping out into the moist air.

The car pulled away as I approached the

door, and I could hear the back bumper nudge one of the trash cans on the curb. Mom was a notoriously bad driver, which my father had always blamed on shear carelessness and she had always claimed to be another example of her free spirited nature. I could tell by the look on Miss Anderson's face as they pulled out of the driveway that she had been reluctant to seat herself in a vehicle with Laura Baker at the wheel. I pressed my thumb to the doorbell and looked around the porch. To my right was a white bench swing, on top of which a magazine was lying face down, its pages flapping open every so often with the cool breeze. Behind

74

the swing I could see the boardwalk off in the distance, where people lugging beach umbrellas and coolers were already beginning to swarm in hopes of getting a good spot on the sand. As if there was such a thing as a bad spot.

After a few moments, the door opened. Behind it stood Scott Anderson.

"Maddie," he smiled, flashing a collection of magnificently white teeth. His brown hair was cut half an inch above his hazel eyes, drawing my glance to the little scar just below his right eyebrow. It had been formed the summer after I was in seventh grade and he was in his freshman year of high school when he had slipped during a junior surfing showcase and banged his head on his board. The wound had once extended to his temple, but had since receded to the point where it was hardly noticeable unless you were looking for it. He wore a light green t-shirt and khaki board shorts, paired with worn out, tan flip-flops.

"Hi, Scott," I replied, smiling back. It was almost surprising to see that he was even slightly happy, given the circumstances. But that was Scott. Always optimistic, always looking on the bright side. We had known each other for my entire life and most of his, and saw one another often when I lived in The Grove, as he was the brother of one of my best friends.

"Please, come in. Faith is upstairs." he said, stepping aside so I could walk in. From what I could tell, the front room was just as I remembered it: a spacious foyer painted light beige with a chandelier hanging above. Ahead were the stairs, which were slightly spiral and lead to the floor with most of the bedrooms, all except Faith's. As Scott and I made our way up the stairs I could see a light shining down from the room on the third floor. Faith's bedroom, as I remembered it, was up the small second flight, which was comprised of about four or five stairs. She was never awfully worried about privacy, therefore the space opened up just at the top of those stairs and was not secluded from the outside by any door. It was a room that had probably been a den or living room of sorts to the house's previous owners, but Faith had chosen to move into it at around twelve years old because she loved the large windows and all the open space.

At the top of the stairs, I began to walk in the direction of the second flight of stairs up to the third floor, up to Faith's room.

"Maddie," Scott said just before I placed my

foot on the first step.

I swiveled around to face him.

"Faith's room isn't up there anymore," he said, motioning toward the hallway to his right. "She made the switch a couple months after you left."

"Oh," I said, turning to walk in the direction he motioned to.

We made our way down the hall, passing his room and the guest bedroom until stopping at the door at the end, which led to the bedroom Faith had as a young child. Scott reached to open the door, then stopped. He turned around to face me.

"Thanks for being here, Maddie."

I nodded.

He reached for the door again and began to open it. I noticed that the knob must have been replaced, as there had once been one with a lock, which Faith and I would use whenever we told each other secrets as little kids. This one had no lock. When the door opened, the first thing I saw was the wall ahead of us. It was pink, a color I knew Faith had never been awfully fond of. The color that it had been ever since the days we'd spent playing with Barbie dolls. The room was dark aside from the light of a small lamp beside the door and that which came off of the television screen in the back left corner of the room.

"Faith?" Scott said, reaching around me to flip up the light switch. When he did, the room came into full view. It was mostly bare, with a bed in the middle, a small night stand, and a dresser, above which hung the flat screen TV. The walls were empty, as was the bed.

"In the bathroom." a voice called from behind the door on the right wall. The sink began to run.

"Someone's here to see you," he replied.

The sound of the running faucet came to a

halt. My heart began to pound lightly as the door opened.

The figure that stepped out was not that of the girl I once knew. She stood in the doorway of her bathroom in a baggy red sweatshirt and black shorts, out of which were two pale, stick-like legs. Her light brown hair was pulled up into a slightly greasy ponytail on top of her head. I became extremely anxious almost instantly and reached for my pocket, sticking two fingers in to feel for the folded paper inside. I sighed with relief upon realizing that it was still there.

"Maddie."

She knows. How does she know? Oh my God. She must hate me.

The figure moved quickly toward me and she wrapped her arms around me, resting her chin on my shoulder. I let out a breath and closed my eyes.

"Faith." I said, holding back tears until the pressure was too much to stand and they began to roll over the edges of my eyelids.

I was sixteen again as I stood there holding my best friend. The two years we spent apart could no longer divide us as we hugged. Our bodies shook as we both cried softly, our tears staining each other's shirts. I knew who she thought of, because he was suddenly dominant in my own thoughts. The other piece of the whole. And the thought of him tightened our embrace, as though Todd Maguire himself was holding the two of us in his own arms.

Letter #8

Dear Todd,

You were so beautiful.

~Faith

Chapter Six

"I can't believe you're finally here," Faith was smiling softly with the same intensely white teeth I remembered. It was as though that was the one aspect of her being that had not been affected by past events and sorrow; a beautiful safe haven for that which could not be touched. "I've missed you so much."

"I've missed you too," I echoed, adjusting myself in the wooden seat. The two of us sat across from each other at her kitchen table, glasses of pink lemonade in front of us. Scott had poured it when we came downstairs while Faith went to the table to sit down. From where I sat I could hear the TV in the living room on the other side of the entrance to the kitchen, but could not see what he had put on from in front of the side wall that separated us. I faced Faith, who was running her pointer finger along the edge of her glass and watching me intently.

"What?" I asked, becoming self-conscious immediately upon recognizing her stare.

"I didn't think you'd really come. They said you were going to last year, but…" she trailed off.

"Oh, right."

The Summer before my senior year of high school, one year after leaving The Grove, I had decided for a brief period of time that I wanted to go back to Jersey for a while. I made the arrangements, calling my mom and breaking the news to my dad, and by mid-July most of my bags were already packed and I was ready to go right then and there. Which I would have, had it not been for a piece of paper I found while emptying the bottom drawer of my dresser a week before my planned departure.

"Sorry about that," I said, downing a sip of my lemonade.

"Don't be," she replied quickly. "I wouldn't have wanted to come back. I would have left too, if I could've. No one ever blamed you for wanting to get away, Maddie. Especially not me."

I shook my head. "You needed me here, Faith. I could never ask you to forgive me for leaving you after what happened with Todd."

She flinched. I wondered immediately if I wasn't supposed to mention his name around her.

"I'm sorry," I said quickly. "I shouldn't have…"

"No." she responded softly. "No, it's okay."

I bit my lip and looked down at my shoes,

an old pair of blue and white running sneakers.

"Madison," Faith said after a moment. I looked up at her, taking note of the slick strings of hair dangling around her face. Strings that had once been locks of beautiful hair. "You don't need to ask. There's nothing to forgive."

You have no idea.

For a few minutes we sat together, taking occasional sips of our lemonade and watching miniscule droplets of rain accumulate on the window beside the table. The Anderson kitchen was set up very similar to my mom's: a large table on the far wall, tall white cabinets and plenty of floor space. Their biggest window was slightly smaller than ours and extended across the entire wall beside the table.

I pulled my cell phone from my pocket and checked the clock on the little screen, which read 12:45 p.m.

"Maddie?" Faith said after a while.

"Yeah?"

"What made you come back this time?"

I smoothed my thumb over my glass, wiping off a thin layer of condensation. It was an awfully good question. What had drawn me back to The Grove after all this time? I could have easily told my mom that I wasn't up to it. Upon first considering the answer, I drew a blank.

"I don't know." I said, biting my lip. "I mean, I missed you."

"That's not why you came back, though."

Faith was always doing this. Ever since we were little, she always seemed to be one step ahead of my own thoughts.

"How do you know?" I asked defensively.

Faith became quiet and we simply watched each other. *Of course I know; I'm your best friend.* her gaze seemed to say. And it was true. Time changes so many aspects of our lives from the time we are young to the time we are not, but not true friendship. That either continues or lingers for as long as we live.

We spoke very little after that. I ran my pointer finger over the rim of my glass and silently came up with every excuse I could give to explain why there was absolutely no way I could stay in The Grove. Each of them was cornier and more contrived than the last; homesickness, missing my friends back in the city, etcetera. I wondered how Mom would react upon my telling her that I couldn't stay. That would be the more difficult part. I looked up at Faith and felt my stomach turn,

93

wishing I would never have to bear the sight of the one I had betrayed in the most horrible of states ever again.

By the time Scott came back in the kitchen it was already around 2:15 p.m. It was almost as though simply being around each other caused time to speed up.

"Just got off the phone with Mom," Scott said to Faith as he pulled a can of soda from the fridge. "She wanted to remind you of some doctor's appointment you have at three. She said she'd drop you off on her way to a client's house."

"Oh, right. Okay." Faith said without

looking up from her glass.

I slowly began to stand. "I should probably go, then." I said.

Scott looked toward me. "You're not walking home in this," he said, gesturing to the window.

"It's no big deal." I replied plainly.

He shook his head. "Let me give you a ride."

I began to insist that I walk home in order to save him the trouble, but his eyes seemed to beg that I cooperate.

So I did.

*   *   *

"You really don't have to," I said as I pulled open the front door and stepped outside. The rain had subsided a little, now only lightly dusting the neatly cut green grass with moisture. Residents of The Grove were very particular about their landscaping, always looking to have the most gorgeous flowers and the greenest grass. This made the town especially spectacular after every rainfall, feeding the exotic plants with life and intensifying their colors as if to mock the hard gray sky with their impeccable beauty.

"It's no big deal," Scott replied, digging into his pocket and plucking out a ring with three or four keys and a miniature novelty surfboard as we stepped down onto the walkway. I looked toward the empty driveway quizzically, and Scott took notice.

"I'm parked out on the curb." he explained, motioning to the tall hedge that blocked any view of the sidewalk and half of the road in front of it.

"Mind if I ask why?" I replied, still confused. The driveway was awfully spacious, certainly big enough to fit the two cars their parents

owned as well as his. There was a garage as well,
but I knew that it was reserved for the antique car
Mr. Anderson had been storing there since we were
little.

"You'll understand when you see her." Scott
laughed.

I couldn't remember him having a car back
when I still lived in The Grove. It never really
struck me as odd, though, even for a senior guy.
Scott practically lived at the beach, and with that
only a few blocks away, there weren't a whole lot
of other places to go. I assumed he had gotten it
before he went off to Balacksrun University, a

school up in North Jersey that he had been talking about wanting to attend for as long as I could remember. Had I ever congratulated him for getting in?

We walked down to the edge of the driveway and turned right on the sidewalk.

"Oh, my God," I said, shaking my head and smiling.

In front of us sat one of the most badly beaten-up pick-up trucks I had ever seen. The back was dented, the bumper hung off a little on the left. The faded green paint was chipped to reveal layers of rust that seemed to have been years in the making. It was old, certainly not an antique by any means but still an old car, especially by the standards of one of the wealthiest towns on the Jersey Shore.

"This is your car?"

Scott smiled, his expression dripping with pride. "Sure is. What do you think?"

We walked around to the passenger's side. I ran my palm over the side of the truck, lightly drumming my fingers over the bumpy exterior. I didn't know what to think.

"My mom hates her," he said, patting the truck with his hand. "Won't even let me park her in the driveway, since she doesn't want to ruin the house's image or whatever. A friend of mine over in Ranson inherited her after his uncle passed away and he was going to send her to the dump until I made an offer. Couldn't resist, I think she has character."

"That's for sure." I laughed. "Does *she* have a name?"

He blushed at my calling attention to his personification of the car. "No. Not yet, at least."

I nodded. Scott unlocked the door with his key and walked around to the driver's side. I stepped up inside the car and adjusted myself in the warm cracked-leather seat.

We took a more complicated route back to my house than necessary, and I'd look over at him occasionally with the expectation that he'd say something. It wasn't until we were pulling up on the curb of Ocean Avenue outside the house that he finally spoke.

"It's worse than it looks." he said, patting the steering wheel. "It looks like a miracle that she can still run, doesn't it? But she's a pretty bad wreck under the hood. We've put so much effort into her, but sometimes it just isn't enough."

I nodded, realizing then that he was not only

referring to the nameless car.

"I can try to help."

"Yeah." he said, his eyes fixed on the stretch
of road ahead. "Yeah, I'd appreciate that, Maddie."

Letter #32

Dear Todd,

Time is such a strange concept. We all lost you at the same time. We all had the same first moments with the knowledge that you were gone and the same first day without you. And over time, they've all moved away from that day. They've all left your memory behind with every other tragedy of the past. And while I know that time has driven a gap between myself and your memory, I can't say that such a wedge has left me any room to feel content. Each day I am left further from the initial

pain of your parting, but each day I am left at a

similar distance from the answers I've so

desperately longed for.

    Time has done me a bitter favor.

~Faith

Chapter Seven

It was as though his words had ignited something within me. The excuses I had conjured for my anticipated sudden departure from The Grove dissipated, leaving room for a longing.

I could not change what had been done.

But I could change Faith.

There was a note on the door from Mom, who had scribbled down that the sale she was having at *Timeless* was a big hit with a large tour group of Asian families and she'd be going out with some of her employees for dinner to celebrate the successful kick-off to the Summer season. I crumpled the note in my hand and made my way toward the kitchen to toss it in the trash. When I did, I noticed a small yellow spiral-down notebook lying on the counter. I opened to the first page and ran my eyes over its contents:

~Eggs

~Milk

~Mineral Water

It was the only page that had been written on in the book. I turned it back and opened to the fresh, white page behind it, then scavenged through the drawers beneath the counter before coming across a blue pen with the name and logo of a local bank inscribed across it.

Upstairs, the door to my room had been left open as Mom had to have gone in earlier to change the sheets and leave a little box wrapped in pink and white paper on the end of the bed. I set the notebook and pen down on the floor beside my feet and carefully unwrapped the box to find that it contained a little watch with a band made up of tiny silver doves. The face of the watch was surrounded by miniscule sparkling jewels.

It was the latest edition to *Timeless*, as I had learned while flipping through one of the monthly catalogs she sent me a few days prior to my leaving the city. I slipped the watch on my wrist and admired it for a few moments before picking up the pen and paper and making my way out to the balcony.

I sat down on the floor of it and began to paint the lined notebook paper in slick, black ink. Words poured from the tip of the pen as though they were in a rush to be liberated from the seclusion of the little plastic tube within. Words were crossed out, scribbled upon, underlined, circled a couple times, then folded within a crumpled paper and tossed to the ground around my crossed legs. My hands occasionally wandered to the paper in my pocket where they would rest for a few moments before coming up with something new to write down.

By the time I was finished, four balls of paper had taken residence in the space around me and one sat on my lap. It, too, was full of scribbles and lines across words. But it bore something that the others didn't. It bore something that the paper in my pocket lacked.

Hope.

*   *   *

"Maddie?" a voice drifted into my subconscious.

I opened my eyes to see Mom hovering over me, the rim of her floppy white sunhat blocking out the light emitted from the lamp she'd turned on beside the couch.

"Awful early to be falling asleep." she chuckled, ruffling my hair the way she did when I was little.

I sat up and looked toward the clock on the wall above the mantle which read 6:37. I then remembered falling asleep in the living room a few hours prior. Mom made her way toward the kitchen, asking if I had eaten anything.

"No, I'm not really hungry." I said, rubbing my eyes. "I thought you were going to be out late?"

"Trying to get rid of me?" she teased from the other room. "There was a last minute rush at the store so I thought I'd stop home before we went out so I could see you. Angie told me she'd take care of it and lock up."

"Ahh."

I reached into my pocket to find the two papers folded neatly on top of each other. The one in back was wrinkled and torn, while the one in front was smooth and crisp. This made me smile a little.

I slipped out the one in front and opened it, scanning the words for what had to have been the seventh time since they'd been written.

"What's that?" Mom asked as she walked back into the room, granola bar in hand.

"A list." I said, pausing before I realized how vague the statement was. "I was trying to think of places I could take Faith before I leave. You know, places we always used to go to before…"

An urgent ting-ing noise erupted from the

phone in her pocket and she held up her pointer finger to me, mouthing the word "sorry" before she stepped out onto the back patio to take the call.

I stood up from the couch and stretched before making my way toward the kitchen to get my own phone, which I had left on the charger upon arriving home. When I flipped it open, the blank screen indicated that I hadn't missed any calls or messages. I opened the contact list and scrolled down to the Anderson's home phone, pressing down on the little green call button.

"Hello?"

"Hi, Mrs. Anderson. It's Madison."

114

"Maddie," I could hear her smiling into the receiver. "Do you want me to get Faith?"

"That'd be great, thanks."

There was silence for a few moments before she came back on the phone.

"I'm sorry, dear, but she's a little preoccupied at the moment. Can I take a message?"

I almost sighed with relief, but somehow stifled the urge to do so.

"Yeah, could you just ask her if she would be interested in going out tomorrow?"

"Of course she would!" she responded ecstatically, immediately assuming the decision-making position.

"Awesome. Do you think she could be ready at around five-thirty am?"

There was a small pause in conversation and I could tell that she was wondering if she should ask why meeting at such an early hour was necessary or let it be due to her enthusiasm over Faith's leaving the house.

"Yes, that shouldn't be a problem."

Let it be.

We said our goodbyes and hung up. When I set down the phone and looked up at the window above the kitchen sink, a piece of my reflection took on a rather odd shape; a shape that I knew I'd once been accustomed to but hadn't considered familiar in a long while.

Peering back into my hazel eyes, a girl wore a small smile.

Letter #42

Dear Todd,

Sometimes I like to believe that hope is real,

even for somebody like me.

~Faith

Chapter Eight

"Good morning." I said as my foot met the hard wood at the bottom of the stairs.

Mom was standing beside the door with a stack of papers in her hand. It had always been her ritual to wake up far more early than the majority of the population of The Grove in order to get in time for morning meditation before work. She had a seemingly perplexed look on her face as she was examining what looked to be in-voices from *Timeless*, a look that only strengthened upon my revealing that I, too, was awake at five o'clock in the morning.

"What are you doing up?" she asked,
adjusting the papers in her hand so that they were
even.

Outside the window, the Sun was just barely
peeking its head above the edge of the boardwalk.
The bike rack on the sidewalk across the street was
empty. The lights above Ocean Avenue had yet to
flicker off.

"I'm taking Faith out today."

"It's hardly five am." she stated quizzically
as we made our way into the kitchen.

"Exactly," I said, opening the door of the

refrigerator and scavenging for orange juice, "Faith won't go somewhere if she thinks she might see someone she knows, so I thought I'd take her to the beach. Who's going to be at the beach at five am?"

I reached into the back and pulled out a half-empty carton, then grabbed a glass from the cabinet above the sink and sat down at the table.

"Ahh," Mom responded, her nose still buried in the papers. She had never been much of a businesswoman; the initial finances that involved opening *Timeless* had all been handled by my dad back when I was hardly old enough to stand.

After downing the orange juice, I said my

goodbyes and started out the door.

"Maddie?" Mom called after me before I stepped outside.

I swiveled around, my navy blue flip-flops making a soft squeaking noise on the hard wood.

"Yeah?"

"Do you want to drive, or…?" she held up her car keys and my stomach turned a little.

"No, that's okay. I'll just get my bike out of the garage."

Sure enough, by the time I had entered the pass-code into the garage and turned on the light inside, there sat my beach cruiser; a cherry red bicycle with little white flowers painted across the exterior, the silver between the handlebars slightly faded from where friends had once hopped on for rides. I ran my fingers over the smooth leather seat and hopped on.

*   *   *

"Faith." I smiled.

She wore a white pair of sweatpants and a tan, zip-up hoodie. Her hair was pulled up into a messy brown bun atop her head, revealing the ever-thin frame of her small face. It was then that I came to notice how much shorter she was than me, at least four or five inches, as if she hadn't grown at all in the years I was gone. This brought me back to the memory I had of our first and last fight in the ninth grade. She and Todd had just begun dating at the time, and I could remember accusing her of having changed. In actuality, this wasn't the case at all. Situations changed, relationships changed, even I changed. But not Faith. Faith was constant.

"Where to?" she asked, her hands buried into the pockets of the hoodie. Her expression let on that she was open to anything, though her eyes suggested otherwise.

124

I looked right toward the end of the slightly winding road, catching sight of the empty boardwalk in the distance, and motioned toward this route to the beach.

"Where else?" I said lightly, and she smiled a little in response.

The walk to the beach was awkward in a great many ways. Faith had apparently let her bike alone for the past couple of years for reasons she didn't state and I didn't ask, so we decided in favor of taking it on foot. This made for a sum of time I hadn't been counting on, time that should have been filled with casual conversation, as it would in an

ideal word, but was instead spent speechlessly
counting the cracks in the sidewalk. She seemed to
be walking more slowly than I considered ordinary,
which I initially shrugged off as the result of my
having become so accustomed to fast-pace city life.
But as we came closer to the boardwalk, it became
clear that her hesitation was contributive to our lack
of speed.

"Are you sure you don't want to walk
around a little more?" she asked, her eyes on our
slowly stepping feet.

"We can walk on the beach." I said, trying
to sound adamant without being too aggressive.

Scott had made it clear that this would take effort, and I had made it clear that I was willing to put as much of that as I had into it.

She nodded, and as she did I looked into her eyes, beginning to hear the words they silently screamed. Pity began to take hold of my judgment.

"I mean, if you really don't want to…" I trailed off.

"No," she said quickly, "it's fine."

We proceeded down the road until the corner of Fraigle Street and Ocean Avenue was beneath our feet.

I looked both ways down either side of the

street and crossed, only to realize upon my reaching

the curb that Faith still stood behind me on the other

side. I had assumed she would follow, but instead

she simply stood, biting her lower lip. It seemed as

though she was miles away, hovering like a

phantom in the world I had already left behind.

"Faith." I called, motioning for her to cross.

She hesitated, staring all the while at the floor of the

road as though there were instructions inscribed in

the pavement.

After a few moments she looked back up at

me, her lips in the shape of an "o" as she released a

slow breath and made her way toward the

boardwalk. I thought about how much easier it would be to take her by the hand and bring her back home. Why did I have to be the one to save her? What made her well-being my responsibility? These questions caught the passing breeze and took flight from my mind the moment I came to recall the tattered old paper in my pocket.

We sat on the beach for a while, our bodies slowly sinking into the cool sands as the Sun took tiny steps up a slightly cloud-dusted pink and blue staircase.

"You really don't have to go to all this trouble for me." Faith said softly, her words melodious with the lightly whining wind that passed at that moment.

I looked over at her, pushing a lock of hair behind my ear. Before I could respond or so much as come up with an appropriate response, she continued.

"Don't get me wrong. I mean, I love that you're here. I just don't think I deserve it, after everything."

I narrowed my brow in confusion.

"Faith, what are you…" I began before she cut me off.

"The special treatment, Madison. You, my

parents, Scott, all treating me like I'm a victim, or something. I didn't do anything to deserve any of it after what I did."

What she did.

Her words traveled down through my body and squeezed the contents inside, strangling my innards and shattering the barricade I'd built around my guilt. The conversation brought me back to the rumors, the lies spread about what happened that night.

"Faith, how could you say that?"

She looked at me as though a second head had popped out of my ear.

"I broke him, Madison. I loved him, and I broke him."

I took a breath. "Faith, he broke up with you. You know that. You and I both know that."

"You weren't there." she snapped before her voice mellowed down a bit, deluded by a sad, guilty tone. "It was such a long time ago. I probably don't even remember right."

"You're not the reason he…"

"How do you *know* that, Madison?" her voice raised again.

It wasn't exactly an argument; not by typical standards, at least. Her tone was more desperate than it was confrontational, as if she didn't have it in her to put forth anything more.

"I'm sorry." I said, though I shouldn't have.

There was no reason for me to apologize, but sometimes you have to substitute pride and judgment for people when that's what they need. That was what Faith needed. She had heard what people said, and all the words that implied that she had broken up with Todd and caused his so-called impulsive decision to end his life had caught up to her. All the blasphemy had finally convinced her that she was responsible for Todd Maguire's act.

Faith nodded and turned her gaze back on

the rolling waters. Her eyes seemed to look

elsewhere, though. I looked in the same direction,

scanning the empty horizon in an attempt to locate

what she saw. It was a few moments later that I

realized trying to was pointless as doing so was

impossible. I couldn't wear her perspective.

*   *   *

The layer of light smeared across the beige

floor surrounding us brightened slowly until every

bird and dune and abandoned flip-flop was painted

a lighter shade. As we were more intensely

illuminated, I could feel Faith becoming anxious.

With light would come tourists with oversized umbrellas and disposable cameras; young children with red pales and shovels. Elderly women armed with interior design magazines and jumbo bottles of sunscreen.

With light would come the familiar faces of those who Faith could not bear to see, so we were only there for about an hour before it was time to head home.

Letter #36

Dear Todd,

This will be the last time I ever write to you.

I'm leaving tonight. I can hear Mom

downstairs, laughing at whatever show is on TV.

Scott is out with friends to see the midnight

premiere of some movie I've never heard of. Dad is

on a business trip down in Washington. I'll have to

make my escape before Mom comes up to bed. It's

ten thirty now, so I should have plenty of time.

There's nothing left for me here. I can't

stand how much it hurts my mom to see me like this,

I can't stand to watch her suffer because of me.

Mom, if you're reading this, please don't blame

yourself for what I'm about to do. You are so

amazing, but I am not worth the pain I've put you

through. Tell Scott and Daddy that I love them,

please. Things will be easier without me around, I

just know it. You'll be sad at first, but things will get

better for you. They didn't for me, because I didn't

deserve to feel better after what I did to you, Todd. I

didn't deserve to move forward.

I can't fight it anymore. It's getting late, so I

better make this quick. This letter will be at the very

top of the pile. Throw it out when you're done

reading it. Try and forget. Try and move on. I want

that for you.

   Goodbye.

~Faith

Chapter Nine

After I dropped off Faith, I hopped on my bike and rode back in the direction of Ocean Avenue. While I pedaled, my eyes maintained a continual fixation on the sidewalk beside me, where spirits of past occurrence loomed so apparently that I nearly reached out to touch the soft head of my younger self, who still seemed to leap in small increments over rudely drawn hopscotch boxes on the concrete.

What remained of that morning was spent at home, flipping through re-runs and scavenging in the pantry. Mom called around noon to see if I was interested in going out to lunch with her and a couple of her coworkers, a request which I politely denied in the interest I suddenly developed in riding my bike around town. She asked how Faith was, to which I responded with the word *good* as it was safe and cut the time that stood between myself and the previously mentioned bike ride.

*   *   *

Each tree, each bench, each table and chair in the windows of the better cafés and diners was a piece of it. A piece of the monument that was The

Grove, the statue sculpted of my childhood. I

pedaled down Main Street, where the sidewalk was

crowded in a sea of lunch-goers and gift shop

visitors. It was clear to me that the chances of

someone out of the bunch recognizing me were

fairly high, but I didn't mind. It was as though I

found myself back in the past; back in a time when

riding my bike down the center of town was an

action that went without second thought.

"Madison! Madison Baker!"

I eased back my right pedal and stopped

beside the curb in front of *Nook & Cranny*, a little

odds and ends shop placed in the basement beneath the old Victorian-style home of the store's owner, then twisted around to look back.

"I *told* you it was her, Den'! I *told* you!" said a girl with bleach blonde hair and a rounded face with a slightly orange tint, probably the result of an expensive spray tan with a cheap-looking outcome. She held a half-eaten sugar cone wrapped in a chocolate-spotted napkin at the bottom.

"Bridget?" I hopped off my bike and wheeled it toward where the two stood.

"How *are* you?" she exclaimed, giving the lanky red-haired boy her ice cream to hold while she pulled me into a hug, wrapping her arms loosely around my neck.

Bridget Trivals.

Bridget and I became fairly close around the time Faith and Todd became close toward the end of eighth grade. She was hired to work the register at *Timeless* and we'd often go out to eat or lay out on the beach for a while after work. She knew me during a period in which I was often alone due to the lessening invitations to go out made by my closest two friends. She knew me when my group of friends was still fairly tight-knit with the exception of the many acquaintances I'd acquired through my friendship with Todd, who knew and was friendly with pretty much everyone. The boy beside Bridget was Dennis, who happened to be an ex-crush of Faith's from elementary school, though I was fairly certain he didn't know it.

"It has been *so* long!" Bridget cooed, fluttering her thickly painted lashes in the direction of the cone in Dennis' hand. He passed it back to her and she bent down to kiss his hand in thanks.

I smiled, reaching back my foot to release the kickstand of my bike so that I could let go of the handlebars.

"I heard you were coming back," she

continued at a rapid pace, reminding me of her

chatty nature, "don't you remember, Denny? Jordyn

said she was. Remember?"

Dennis nodded.

She smiled wide, revealing the

magnificently bright army of pearls that were quite

obviously whitened on an unhealthily regular basis.

"When did you get here?"

"Couple days ago." I replied lightly.

Despite the many rumors I could recall

hearing about Bridget, I had always liked her. It was

a liking similar to that had by Faith when she

encountered people with sketchy reputations but

evidently good qualities; a liking that she couldn't help but have for those who couldn't always project the light within them through their actions.

"And you haven't stopped by to say hello even once!" she belted, immediately releasing a laugh to follow the statement.

I apologized between semi-sincere giggles.

"God, it has to have been two *years* now. What brought you back after all this time?"

I opened my mouth to speak, but not a sound was emitted.

Dennis tapped Bridget's arm with the back of his fingers and she looked up at him with a baffled expression, as though she was caught in the middle of some sort of inside joke. He looked at her, making a face that reflected on how uncomfortable he must have felt as he said the name.

"Faith."

"Oh." Bridget shaped her mouth in a slight 'o' then bit her bottom lip in embarrassment. "I'm sorry, Madison. I totally forgot."

They spoke of Faith as though she was the victim of a horrendous murder or the casualty of some other tragedy. They spoke of Faith as though she was Todd. This was incredibly rare, as it contrasted with the opinions of Faith held by the majority of those who knew well of the incident and the parties involved.

"No," I said, "it's fine. She's out of the hospital, she seems to be better than I heard she was. She's eating again, too."

The two exchanged a look.

"So she hasn't..." Bridget began slowly as if testing the waters in case she was asking a question that required a response with too much confidential detail. "...tried again?"

I furrowed my brow. "Tried..."

She leaned back her head to share another

look with Dennis, her eyes screaming an S.O.S. into his.

"She means…Faith hasn't tried to, you know, kill. Herself…again." he said in a low voice.

I snapped into silence and relocated my sight, though certainly not my attention, to the ground below my feet.

"I…I thought you knew." Bridget stuttered.

A wave of humiliation shot through me as I realized then how little I knew. It was an emotion that mixed with anger toward Mom and Mrs. Anderson for having never shared this information with me, as if I couldn't handle it after what happened with Todd.

"I, um, I didn't. When? When did she…" I

trailed off, looking back up at them.

"It was why she went to the hospital."

Dennis said, and I remembered then that he lived

across the street from Faith. I could imagine the

sirens; the ambulances galloping down the road just

as they had two years ago, their riders likely in

silent prayer that the two outcomes would bear no

similarity. This image made it more difficult for me

to convince myself that what they said was the

result of rumors and mistaken information as I

realized that he had probably witnessed it all from

the comfort of his home.

The limit of my ability to ask about what happened with Faith and accept that the answers would be true was hit before I could question *how* she had tried. I never came to regret not knowing her method of choice, though.

We spoke for a little while longer on unrelated subjects including some banter about how we should all get together before I left. Even at the time I knew that it was pretty far from likely that I'd see them again while I was there unless such a meeting were to again occur by chance, but I nodded and agreed anyway. Faith's name didn't come up again, though it hung stagnant in the air until we said our goodbyes and parted ways.

I spent what remained of that day riding my bike around town, whizzing past all that I had once known to be familiar with a perspective that skewed such familiarity. Just when darkness began to settle upon the rooftops and pavements of The Grove, I found myself at the Anderson residence.

Letter #127

Dear Todd,

Maybe we're all just moving in circles. That would explain why everything comes back around.

That would mean you'd come back. That would mean all the riches of living in an unknowing state of mind beneath the blanket of youth would come back and warm those who've grown too knowledgeable, too, but neither will happen. You can't rid yourself of the lessons you've learned or the information you've obtained, the same way you can't undo the things you might regret, if you're still alive to regret them. And that's where the circle

153

breaks. We either pry for the things we never should

have wanted to begin with or we make a decision

that just plain isn't right.

~Faith

Chapter Ten

"Hey, Scott."

Scott opened the door and gave a smile weaker than any I'd ever seen painted across his face. "Maddie, I didn't think we were expecting you. What's up?"

Before I could answer, Mr. Anderson came up from behind him with a weary expression. He was dressed in a full suit with a red, diamond print tie; he had probably just returned from work. His eyes widened upon seeing me in the doorway.

"Madison Baker!" he said with a grin,

moving around Scott to get a good look at me. "How've you been?"

"Good, Mr. Anderson. How are you?"

"Well," he looked around his shoulder and gave a slight shrug, "you know. But I'm just fine, I suppose. Sorry to run, but I've got a conference call in a couple minutes so I'd better head upstairs. We'll have to have you for dinner one of these nights while you're in town."

I nodded and thanked him as he receded back into the house, then turned my attention back on Scott, who had his head twisted back in an anxiously awkward position, as if he was waiting for the space behind him to suddenly implode.

"Is everything okay? I could always come back or call later if this is a bad time."

"What?" he said, stirring from whatever thought had been grasping his mind. "No. I mean, it's fine. What did you need?"

My intent upon arriving at the Anderson household was to remind Faith of the plans I'd told her of for the next day without mentioning what Dennis and Bridget had told me. This intent dripped from my memory upon standing there in front of Scott, leaving me with no actual reason as to what compelled me to interrupt what seemed to have been an evening that was already on a downward spiral.

Just when I was on the cusp of telling him to forget about it, a wail erupted from upstairs. Scott winced, but didn't look back. Instead, he took gentle hold of my elbow and guided me out onto the porch, shutting the door behind him.

"I'm sorry." he said.

"Don't be." I replied softly as he made his way to the bench swing and sat down, where he leaned over to rest an elbow on his thigh and rubbed at the space around his temple in a helpless manner.

I sat down beside him slowly, unsure of

whether or not he wanted me to.

"Is it something I said to her? Is it because of what she and I talked about?"

Scott looked up at me with a perplexed look on his face as he probably momentarily wondered what our conversation had consisted of, then said, "No. It's not, Madison. You can't take it personally. It's just Faith."

In my mind I could see Faith crying up in her practically empty bedroom, holding her face in a pile of blankets as she screamed. Mrs. Anderson was probably up there too, consoling her.

"When she went to the hospital," I said

slowly, "it wasn't just because she wasn't eating."

He shook his head and I could tell he wasn't surprised that I'd found out.

"I always thought I knew Todd." Scott said, and I noticed then that there were tears rolling down his cheeks, dripping onto his navy blue shirt as his head remained tilted toward the ground. "When he and Faith started dating, I remember thinking about how lucky I was to have a guy like him looking out for my sister. Told him so once, too."

He sat up and took in a shaky breath, turning his head toward the house so that I wouldn't see him crying.

"Didn't he know how it would affect her? Didn't he think about what this would do to her?" he said in a near whisper.

My stomach tightened and I reached for the paper in my pocket, touching it for only a moment.

"I don't know, Scott. Everybody says that when someone gets the way he did, they just have a hard time thinking about how they'll affect the people they love."

It was then that I realized I wasn't referring to Todd and had to catch myself before I delved further.

"But," I continued, "I don't really think

that's how it was with Todd. I think he wanted what was best for Faith. I think he thought that hurting her before he, you know, would make her miss him less."

Scott looked up.

"Did he do that to you too, Madison?"

I turned my sight toward my shoes and took a breath of the salty air, sucking the warm humidity into my lungs.

"Yeah," I said, "I guess he did."

*　*　*

I asked Scott to remind Faith of our plans

for the next day before I left. By the time I was home, I could see that Mom's car was parked in the driveway. I put away my bike and came back outside. A few clouds had accumulated in the space above where I stood and after a few moments a light mist began to fall. A gaggle of teenagers sat on and around a bench in front of the boardwalk across the street where they appeared to be playing with a small deck of cards. A few couples and surfers still walked along the boardwalk, their slow steps reflecting on the calm, unrushed atmosphere of The Grove's summer evenings. Tourists with their booming laughs and snapping cameras had already

163

crawled back into the motels they'd come from in neighboring towns. Not a word or snap poured over and broke the silence.

Silence remained silent.

The world took a sigh and closed its eyes, thus enveloping the sight of those who remained awake in darkness. As it did, I remembered all that had once made The Grove my home.

Letter #61

Dear Todd,

There are pieces everywhere. Across the

street there's that big old oak tree beside the

sidewalk in front of the Grimley family's house. The

one we climbed when the three of us snuck out that

night in seventh grade. It was so dark, I could

hardly keep sight of the branches we groped for and

clung to. But you didn't need your eyes, or any

other sense, really. No, you had instinct. But those

branches couldn't hold you, Todd, and Madison

and I had no way to catch you from the high places

we too had reached. The ambulance showed up five

minutes after I called. Seemed like the whole

neighborhood came around us that night after your

fall to watch the blinking lights whisk you away

beneath the wing of a gaggle of quick-footed

paramedics. In the rush of things over the days that

followed, I don't think I was asked what it was like

up there at the top before the fall that stole our

breath and broke your arm.

Maybe you wouldn't have remembered,

anyway. But I could probably describe the entire

night in spot-on detail. Because to me, that tree is a

166

piece of the way things were. Our taste of freedom

had its cost and consequence, but I'd pay a greater

price to make such a memory again, even if that

meant being the one to hit the ground.

~Faith

Chapter Eleven

The Pier was about forty-five minutes away from The Grove. It consisted of long stretches of prize-winning games and several tiki-style bars and restaurants as well as numerous rides, including a miraculously lit Ferris Wheel. It stretched out over the main beach in Allen Arbor, an area teeming with bennies and residents of summer homes. It was for this reason that hardly anyone from The Grove had any interest in visiting it. And for that reason, it was perfect for Faith.

We picked up Faith at around five-thirty in

the afternoon. Mom had offered to drop us off as she had been meaning to visit and attempt to make a client of a woman designing jewelry made from recycled watches out of her home in the area. Scott walked Faith to the car, gently pressing a hand to her shoulder.

I stepped out of the passenger side of the car and came out to open her door for her. I then saw that she wore a lightly colored pair of boot-leg jeans and a navy blue sweatshirt with the words "Best healthcare on the Jersey Shore. Crest Health." It was the slogan for the hospital she had volunteered at weekly since seventh grade. I had forgotten about her having done so until that point, as it was one of those little regularities you forget about when nothing is normal anymore.

My own outfit consisted of a faded yellow tank top and light denim jacket, paired with faded black shorts. Though it was late in the day, the sun's rays still beat down with great intensity, thus leading me to wonder how Faith could possibly stand being dressed so thickly. I didn't ask, though.

When we arrived at The Pier, a crowd of teenagers was beginning to accumulate around the entrance on the boardwalk. Nighttime usually attracted the local adolescent population and sent families with small children packing.

"Have fun," Mom said with a smile. There were shards of caution in her tone, as she was probably almost as nervous as I was. Faith had hardly left her house in the past two years; this occasion marked her first dive into a world she'd avoided all that time.

A world of people, all of whom had the potential to break and be broken.

We walked around the boardwalk for a little while, browsing around the little shops and stands that lined it facing the beach and the ocean. I had silently swore that I would not so much as comment about the crowded pier itself until she either suggested we go or asked that we leave.

"I wonder how old that Ferris Wheel is." Faith said while we were sifting through a rack of heavily beaded sun dresses in a small bohemian-style shop that smelled of incense and rotting wood.

I looked outside the front of the store, which was diagonal to The Pier across the way, giving it a perfect view of the wheel on the far left side.

"I don't know," I said wistfully, racking my brain for an extension to the topic in case she didn't continue talking about it. "I'll bet it's about as old as The Pier."

Faith held a dress up to her torso and cringed, placing it back on the rack. I wondered if her silent criticism was toward the dress or how she thought she'd look in it.

"Probably," she said. "Do you think it's really busy over there?"

"It doesn't look too bad." I said quickly.

Upon doing so I immediately hoped I hadn't sounded too anxious, but Faith didn't seem to notice.

She nodded and picked up another dress, this one a bright yellow.

"Do you want to go?" she asked.

I smiled. "Absolutely."

* * *

The sign above the entrance that read "The Pier" in the form of blinking colored light bulbs always reminded me of a picture my father once showed me when I was young. The picture was of him standing beside his four older brothers beneath a similar sign that read "Buccaneer's Point", which was what The Pier had been called before it was bought out and renovated in the late seventies. In the picture his little twiggy legs are sticking out of a pair of shorts that look two sizes too large and he is wearing a pair of sneakers that look awfully tattered for that of such a young boy, but these were never the things I noticed first upon running my eyes over that particular photograph.

No, the first thing I'd see was his smile. It was one he didn't wear very often even in other candid depictions of his youth. It was one that stuck out more evidently there as he stood in front of the long line of boardwalk games and bumper cars, one that simply emanated joy.

One that simply emanated hope.

Faith and I meandered for about two hours,

occasionally pointing out small children with oversized stuffed animal prizes and the hilariously uncomfortable looks on the faces of people on rides like the tilt-a-whirl. I couldn't help but notice that she'd look away any time we passed spots of significance, places I could remember vividly from our childhood purely due to the fact that they were the locations on which Todd would say or do something we'd later look back on and laugh about with him. It seemed as though his memory was sprouting in abundance from the wood beneath our feet, as though our presence made the atmosphere fertile to recollections of his past existence.

Upon being bombarded by the memories, I wondered if Faith ever knew how mutual our pain was. Probably not.

We had passed the Ferris Wheel a few times before the line was short enough to seem reasonable. This I would not have noticed if Faith hadn't mentioned it.

"Want to get on line?" she had asked, catching me off guard.

In a matter of minutes we were lifted into the air and drawing circles in the sky.

Letter #13

Dear Todd,

You've already moved on. Please, please just let me do the same. Drop out of my dreams, be absent from my thoughts. Your intention was to leave, so why haven't you?

~Faith

Chapter Twelve

The world was small from up there. The ocean was too dark to be seen beneath all the lights, but when I listened hard I could just barely hear the crashing of waves on the shore. We sat on the same side of the seat, leaving the bench closer to the spine of the wheel abandoned. I assumed this was because Faith was nervous for one reason or another. She seemed content though, swinging her legs slightly as the light wind pushed back her hair.

I looked down at the couple beneath us. The girl had her brown hair tied in a loose braid on the side of her neck and a little white flower clip that held back the hair that was too short to be braided. She was sitting beside a boy who had his arm around her shoulder. I watched as she let her head fall back onto his chest as the two looked off in the direction of the water, both bearing subtle smiles. I could see then that Faith was looking too, her eyes appearing to become slightly glassy.

"Hey," I tapped her shoulder with the back of my hand, "remember when we used to throw ice on people from the top?"

Faith looked up, her eyes distant. I smiled, picked up the empty cup of soda I had purchased earlier and shook it, listening to the clanking of the cubes at the bottom. She smiled back.

The wheel stopped when we were a couple spots away from the crest. I popped the plastic top off of my cup and tilted it toward Faith, who hesitantly reached in and retrieved three or four of the gleaming little blocks. I took a few and motioned in the direction of the seat where the couple sat.

"One…" I whispered as though my cue could possibly be heard by those below over the sound of winning game bells and screaming children.

"Two…"

It was at that moment that Faith's eyes opened. Not in the sense that her eyelids lifted, which is to say that it was not in a literal form. It was far more than a literal action ever could be. It was more real. Her corneas burst and split, and from them was poured a light. One that had most definitely dwelled in its place before. One that I'd once known well.

"Madison?"

I stirred from the thought, my eyes still fixed on hers.

"Right," I said, "okay…three!"

We each dropped a cube and threw ourselves back into the middle of the seat in excitement, all the while chirping low, raspy giggles. As soon as I caught my breath, the wheel was turning again, but only for a few moments. I looked down at the couple, who was laughing and scouring the bottom of their seat in attempt to locate what had so mysteriously fallen from the sky. I looked at Faith, who still sat laughing and lightly clapping her hands in glee. The wheel stopped again, this time at the very top.

And Faith and I sat there together, saturated in the frozen moment.

183

Part Two
Faith

Chapter Thirteen

The wheel began to turn again. A familiar ballad boomed from a nearby beanbag- toss game booth as our seat made its way to the ground. People toted trays of cheese-fries and fried oreos toward the picnic area where tables were set up beneath a large white tent. Men standing behind counters at booths whistled as potential customers wandered by, explaining their games quickly in boisterous tones in order to be heard over the many voices stuffed within the thick air.

Life moved around me.

But this time, I was part of it.

"Faith!" Madison called me over from where I stood staring at a hanging array of stuffed bears with big glassy eyes and curved black smiles.

She was beside a small booth lined with red-clothed tables, all of which displayed dazzling assortments of jewelry. I walked over and she showed me a turquoise ring with a seashell-print pattern across the band. As she did, I noticed the table across from us. On it was a glass case.

"You should get that." I said, smiling as she unzipped her purse and dug for cash.

I walked toward the case, beside which

stood a man with a keen eye on all who browsed the tables. Inside were several rows of silver necklaces, all of which bore different names. Alexandra, Annabelle, Anthony...

"Twenty dollars each." he stated in an accent I couldn't quite put my finger on as he watched me scan the necklaces behind the glass.

"Just name a name, I'll probably have it."

I looked back at Madison, who was talking to the other man working at the booth.

"There are three." I said softly, reaching into my pocket for the wad of money Scott had pushed upon me earlier.

*   *   *

I heard bells when we left The Pier. Bells

with a strong enough clatter to be heard above the

commotion behind us and a soft enough sound to

resemble the song poured from the beaks of waking

birds. I turned back for a moment to locate them,

which I was unable to do. The crowd making its

way out swept Madison and I in the direction of the

road, where we would stand and wait for Miss

Baker. But I didn't stop thinking about the bells. In

my mind I could still hear them, loud and clear.

Before I got out of the car upon pulling up beside my house, Madison told me that tomorrow was my choice. She smiled upon saying so, her eyes glistening with what seemed to be no less than a look of victory. It painted over the caution which had resided before it and remained intact for as long as I still sat in the car.

"Whatever you want to do," she said, "whatever you feel like doing."

Scott opened the door for me, his smile wide as he waved at Madison and Miss Baker while they pulled away.

"Hey," he said, leading me in with his hand

behind my back. Doing so was a habit of his ever since I was young, one that strengthened in consistency two years prior.

I pressed my hand against the pocket of my jeans to feel for the little brown package inside as I had worried it might fall out. Thankfully, it was there.

"How was it?" he asked as we moved toward the kitchen.

I realized then that I hadn't said hello, but it was too late. The subtle anxiety in his tone told me that the greeting lacked relevance in comparison to the anticipated description of my night's outcome.

"It was good," I said, "I had fun."

There was a moment of shock. He wasn't the only one who felt it, though. I did, too.

My reply to any question pertaining to the few things I had taken part in in recent years was *fine*. But it was not only that I had extended my adjectives so far as to call something *good* that called for surprise, it was also the statement that had come after that. *I had fun.* And I did. That is exactly what happened. I had a good time. I had fun.

"Did you?" he paused before he asked, probably making a judgment call about whether or not it would be appropriate to point out just how colossal that moment was.

"Yeah." I said, nodding slightly as I poured a glass of lemonade from the pitcher on the counter.

It was almost as though I had come off the Ferris Wheel and stepped into a vortex of commonality. I was a teenage Jersey girl coming home from the boardwalk, where she had been with her friend. I held the glass of lemonade up to my face and took a small sip, then looked into the glass.

My reflection stared back with content eyes and leaned toward me so that I may hear her whisper the word *normality* into my ear.

Letter #16

Dear Todd,

The world is such a different place now, and you haven't even been gone that long. It scares me, thinking about all the things you'll never see again. The things you'll never see at all. Was relief so valuable that you'd trade it for all the new discoveries and experiences you could have had? That won't be me. That will never be me.

~Faith

Chapter Fourteen

The alarm went off at three a.m., and I actually thought about ignoring it for a change. This thought persisted for about thirty seconds.

Outside, the air smelled like salt and grass. I ran my thumb over the flashlight tucked inside my small over-the-shoulder canvas bag in order to be certain that I had remembered it. Not that I ever needed it. The street lights cast a dim orange glow on the pavement beside me, bringing light to the occasional broken pair of sunglasses or empty sunscreen bottle.

My hair was still slightly damp from the shower I'd taken earlier, which made the breeze on my head a little chillier. I pulled up the hood of my soft blue jacket and coaxed my hair out of the hood with my fingers so that it would dry more quickly. I walked in the direction of Main Street, stopping short when I came to Chester's Sweet Stop. There were four fifty-cent candy/prize machines in front of the store, just as there had always been. I reached into my bag and drew eight quarters from what had to have been an accumulation of about a hundred. I dropped the quarters into the slots one by one and turned the knob of the first machine until it clicked. I then watched the plastic capsule drop to its exit and held the little metal door shut so that the prize wouldn't fall out; repeating the process with the other machines before moving on.

I walked a few blocks further before I came upon my spot.

Between the shops on the west side of Main Street and the houses behind them there was a fence. Two fences, actually. A vinyl white one that had been collectively paid for by shop-owners and a slightly shorter wooden brown one that connected with several others bordering the yards of those who lived one street over on Hunt Road. Between the fences was a small gap. A gap where the grass remained low to the ground as it was only sustained by the sunlight that penetrated the slender splits in the fence.

I had come across the gap the first night I slipped out of the house. The white fence had been garnished with a thin string of colorless lights for the holiday season; lights that extended toward the end and trailed down the bottom where they were plugged into an outdoor outlet. The gap itself could not be seen without the lights as it was behind a stop sign located at the corner of Main Street and

Vogal Way.

I slipped back behind the white fence and walked a little ways until I was behind Mary Tiggle's yard. Mary Tiggle was around seventy-three years old with the vivacity of a sugar-engorged toddler. She worked as a European Literature professor at a university in North Carolina for most of the year and came up every summer to live in a house she'd inherited in The Grove. Local professors and scholars always came out of the woodwork when she'd visit, spending long nights having long-winded discussions on her back deck over glasses of wine and champagne.

"It is when we don't *know* who we are that we are vulnerable to change," a woman's voice sounded with enthusiasm as I took a seat on the grass.

"Changing someone who wasn't anyone is hardly change at all. It's more like a rearranging of numbers in a random pattern. Without a solid initial identity, there is no change."

The second voice was Mary's. Though it had been a year since I had last heard her rant drunkenly about philosophy and politics, I had no difficulty distinguishing her passionate, raspy tone.

"I don't know that I can agree with you

there, Mary."

"And why is that?"

"Because not knowing who one is does not mean that one is without an identity. In fact, I wouldn't see it incredibly unfair to suggest that one who knows who they are or claims to actually knows less than one who accepts that they know little."

"Oh?"

"Yes. Due to pride."

"Pride does not make one's knowledge less valid, dear."

The argument rested for a moment before it

picked up again. I reached into my canvas bag and pulled out the little black notebook within it. The notebook's cover was cracked and torn in several places and the spine hardly still held the pages together, which was frustrating as I had only purchased the book a few months prior. I opened it and flipped through toward the back, where I could see that only three or four pages were open to inhabitance. All the others were rigid and coated in ink.

I ran my fingers through the inside of my bag once more and pulled out a thin, blue-ink pen.

"What a *riot*, do you honestly think that

there is any…" Mary and her minions persisted behind me.

I uncapped the pen and began to roll its point over the surface of the paper.

Dear Todd,

Things are changing…

Intellectual word weaponry sliced through the night air; people emitting passion with the anticipation of being disagreed and fought with. But there was a peace in the scene. Perhaps it was not had by the scholars whose discussions I secretly lent ear to, but it was certainly present in me. So I sat and wrote and prayed that my peace would stretch toward the one who had returned it to me. I sat and wrote and prayed that my peace would stretch to Madison.

Dear Todd,

I used to do such wonderful things for the world around me. I used to volunteer, I used to help people. I used to make people happy. Where have I gone, Todd?

Where have you taken me?

~Faith

Chapter Fifteen

"Sand Creek."

Mom closed the pantry door with the bottom of her foot as she made her way across the floor en route to the dishwasher.

"On Main?" she asked, flashing an expression of concern in my direction.

"Yeah, I told her I wanted to go for lunch. She's coming over at eleven."

Sand Creek was one of my favorite restaurants in The Grove as a young child, mainly because I had liked to watch all the older kids, like the teenagers, get together and gossip over breadsticks and sparkling lemon water. Their lives always seemed so interesting, so extravagant and fantasy-like.

"I don't know, Faith." Mom said as she tapped the dishwasher's buttons with her neatly manicured fingertips. "It seems like you're rushing things. I mean, don't get me wrong. I love that you want to go out, especially to a place where odds are you're going to see some people you know."

"Knew." I corrected under my breath.

"But I just don't want you to think that your condition will be back to normal with the snap of a finger. Progress is good when it's taken one step at a time."

"It's just a lunch. I'll see people from town, and people from school, but I can handle that."

"Two weeks ago I could hardly get you to run outside and grab the mail. I just don't want you to push yourself so hard that you'll snap, hon'."

Her tone was exasperated and helpless.

She didn't know that Sand Creek was only a decoy.

"What's the matter?" Dad's voice sounded from the kitchen doorway. He held the daily newspaper beneath his arm and balanced two coffees in his hands, one of which he held out for Mom.

"Nothing," I said, sitting down at the kitchen table, "Madison's taking me out to lunch today."

"Is she?" His face brightened.

Scott had left a pile of papers on the table consisting primarily of summer assignments he had been working on until late into the night before. The paper on top was an outline of topics for an essay he was working on. I moved my eyes over the words across the page once or twice before becoming bored with the unfamiliar content.

"They're going to Sand Creek." Mom said,

sipping what smelled like a spice late`. "What do you think, Al'?"

"What do I think of what?" he asked, sitting across from me at the table and spreading his paper over the space between us.

"My going to Sand Creek." I said softly.

Dad ruffled his brow. "What do you mean 'what do I think'? I think it's a great idea."

A lawnmower sounded outside. Mom plucked a banana from the counter and sat down beside Dad, rolling her eyes at what he had said.

"You don't think it might be too soon?"

She gave a look that screamed the words

211

don't you remember what happened last time? and began to peel the banana.

Last time. My mind reeled backwards and put on a display of flashing pictures, frames of memory from the last time I had thought I was getting better.

Kah-ching.

The cash register had to have been at least fifty years old. Mary-Ellen beat down the keys with the tips of her fingers and ripped a receipt from the side of the machine.

"Thanks for coming to Sun Dove. Have a great day."

The man at the counter nodded his head, opened the door, and stepped outside. As he did, a gust of chilly air swept into the diner and sent goose-bumps up my back.

"Sorry about that, Faith. Somehow you always wind up with the booth by the door." Mary-Ellen said as she moved toward my table, little order-notebook in hand.

I didn't mind the booth by the door. I had a perfect view of the display window at the stained-glass gift store across the way. The colorful glass patterns that hung in the window were less brilliant without the glare of the sun as the shop was located

213

along a back road across from the building in

which Sun Dove was located, thus preventing light

from hitting them, but I still loved to run my eyes

over them and admire their beauty.

"It's fine." I said, smiling a little.

"Okay, can I guess?" she asked.

I closed the brightly colored menu and

placed it in her open hand as she began to recite

her prediction of my order.

"Two eggs, scrambled. Half a grapefruit

with a little bit of sugar sprinkled on top. And

bacon."

Mary-Ellen had worked at the diner since I

was a toddler. By the looks of her, she was probably

in her early forties. She had a grace about her as

she waltzed around Sun Dove balancing plates and

greeting customers, a grace that is had only by a

woman with a certainty in her actions and a

confidence in her pursuit. She was a woman of

strong faith; never missed a day of church. And she

was the reason I didn't mind leaving home every

once in a while on my own. My visits to the

restaurant had become more frequent in the weeks

prior, and at times I would even consider asking if

she was looking to hire some help.

    "Oh, and a glass of orange juice." she

added with a wink. "Which better not be the only

thing you touch."

Aside from the tutor Mom had hired to come

to the house five days a week in the afternoons and

my psychiatrist, Mary-Ellen was the only contact I

had with the world outside my house. It had been

rumored that Madison might be back that summer,

but I didn't plan on getting my hopes up for that

again.

"Thanks," I said, running my pointer finger

over the condensation on the glass of water that had

been set on the table upon my arrival.

She patted my back before swiveling around

on the soles of her sneakers and making her way

toward the two elderly men sitting at the table

behind me.

Steam rolled up from the little pitchers in the

coffee machines.

Bread hopped up from toasters.

The bell above the door made a soft 'clang'

as people came and departed.

Bus boys scrambled over the tiled floor,

large gray bins with piles of plates in their

calloused hands.

A small TV in front of the counter cheerily

informed listeners of the weather forecast for The

Grove and surrounding areas.

A man dressed in a suit with a blood-red tie flipped the pages of his newspaper slowly while taking occasional sips from a beige mug.

Flip, sip, hop, kah-ching.

Clang.

The door opened at the push of a green-gloved hand.

The individual connected to the hand stepped inside.

My hand reached almost immediately for my gut, which had already tied itself in a tight knot. Of all the encounters that could have occurred in the little diner just outside The Grove, this was the most

unbearable. I'd prepared myself for running into

old friends, even running into his *old friends. But*

not Tara Maguire. Not Todd's mom.

The widow of a man who'd passed away

when Todd had hardly learned his first words stood

in the doorway of the diner, her eyes wide as she

got a feel for the Sun Dove. The owner of a business

that had tumbled into turmoil within the past year

due to economic crises was greeted by Mary-Ellen

and smiled at the sight of the vivacious waitress.

And on the way to her table, the mother of a sixteen-

year-old boy who had hung himself in his bedroom

closet stopped short upon noticing the girl who sat

at the booth by the door.

After the incident, Madison had told me that

Miss Maguire never blamed me for what happened

to Todd.

She had cooed on about how Tara had seen

the signs, about how she knew that her son had

been treading down dark waters for a while before

his suicide.

Surely she knew that his death was not my

fault.

By that point, even I had convinced myself

that it wasn't.

Even I found myself writing him less letters and losing less sleep.

Until the woman in the diner spoke.

"I'm sorry." she said to Mary-Ellen, who was already setting down a menu on a table beside the counter for her.

"What's the matter, hon'?"

Miss Maguire opened her mouth to say more, but nothing came out. Her eyes remained fixed on me.

The world teased the circumstances and slowed to a pause so that I may become drenched in the moment. So that I may have enough time to paint myself in guilt and shame once again.

"I've got to go." Tara Maguire said softly
as she rushed out the door.

The memory of my first of three trips to the
hospital was far less vivid as it had been swept into
the recesses of my mind. I could remember the
blood on my hands, the tears in my mother's eyes,
the flickering of white lights as I fought to keep my
eyelids up, and nothing more.

I knew things would be different with my
parents after that. The mind may win at an effort to
push thoughts and memories away, but it is never

totally rid of what the heart holds.

"If she feels up to going, she should go."
Dad said, his eyes still fixed on the newspaper.

The subject had been put to rest. What remained of my time at the table was spent partaking in casual snippets of conversation and listening to Mom list an array of breakfast options for me, all of which I denied. Usually she would have ignored my rejection and made something for me anyway, but this time I was able to argue that I'd be eating with Madison in only a few hours and wanted to keep up my appetite. I cannot be sure of whether or not she believed me, but in any event I was excused and allowed to leave the table without spending half an hour pushing food around a full plate.

After breakfast I felt impelled to walk outside, driven by the fantasy of rolling my toes over the freshly mown grass and soaking in the sunshine that poured over the streets and rooftops of The Grove. I peered out the window beside the front door and noticed a gaggle of girls about Scott's age stopping to take pictures together on the sidewalk across the street.

"I just don't want you to think that your condition will be back to normal with the snap of a
224

finger."

I wrapped my hand around the brass

doorknob and smiled a little.

Letter #17

Dear Todd,

    You're not gone. You can't be, I still feel you here. They've all acknowledged it, even accepted it, but I can't bring myself to do the same. Couldn't you just tell me, give me a warning? At least I'd know you meant to leave, I'd know it wasn't all a big mistake. And maybe I'd stop having that horrible dream. That horrible dream about some wicked, blank-faced man coming into your house and taking your life himself, then setting it up to look like you could have committed such an act on your own.

But sometimes I must admit I wish that was the case, Todd. It would make more sense for you to leave by an act of cruelty from a world that proves its wickedness time and time again than for you to leave at the hand of the one who had me convinced that there were glimmers of light to be seen in every shadow.

~Faith

Chapter Sixteen

"A booth by the window, if you don't mind."

The waitress, a lanky blonde woman with shear white eye shadow, nodded toward Madison and led us to our seats, gently laying two menus on the table as we made ourselves comfortable. Sand Creek was just beginning to fill up, people filed in smelling of saltwater and sunscreen. The restaurant looked the same as it always had, a fairly small, low-lit room with dark paneled walls, on which hung an array of decorative vintage fishing supplies.

228

I had taken the seat closer to the far wall, where I had a perfect view of the door. If I could get through this meal without freaking out, everything would be okay, and the plan I had fabricated the night before would run smoothly. Psychasthenia. That was the word my therapist liked to use when she referred to my breakdowns. If I could walk out the door of the restaurant knowing full well that I did not so much as approach a psychasthenia, the day would be a success.

"Faith?"

My barrier of contemplation shattered and my cheeks burnt a soft red in embarrassment.

"Sorry," I said, "just zoned out."

Madison nodded. Her hair was pulled up into a messy bun from which several strands dangled. She had probably put it up last minute upon feeling how humid it was outside.

"I was wondering what made you choose to come here," she said.

"Is this too much?" I asked quickly in response. A sense of anxiety shot through my spine and I hoped that it hadn't come through in my tone.

"What? No, I love it here. I was just curious."

Why is it that the first few minutes of
230

conversation are always the hardest? I suppose this is when the mood of the speakers participating is established, thus making it possible to decide what topics can be brought up without making one another feel uncomfortable. It was then that I realized how complex the dynamics of human contact truly were. You can know a person your whole life and still find yourself struggling to construct subjects of discussion upon seeing them. But I suppose our situation was somewhat excused in that aspect.

The waitress made her way back to the table with forks and knives wrapped in red cloth napkins in her hands. "What can I get you two to drink?"

After we ordered, the conversing began. Madison remembered a hand game we used to do as little girls and the two of us playfully struggled to recall the lyrics of the song that went with it. I asked her if she was excited for NYU, where I had been told she'd be attending in the Fall. Her response was casual and less enthusiastic than one might anticipate, but I didn't ask why. Simply thinking about her being anywhere else made me uneasy.

"So, no one ever told me if I missed much while I was gone." she said, smiling as she downed a sip of her sparkling water.

"Hardly," I said as though I had any way of answering the question.

My isolation made it difficult to stay updated on the happenings of The Grove, but I loved that she'd asked. Most of the questions people asked me pertained to my current psychological condition, my plans for whatever holiday was coming up, or my shoe size. The last was asked more commonly than you might think. Shoes are the safe gift when you don't know what to get someone. My unwrapping them was nothing less than humorously ironic, though. So many shoes for someone who hardly ever stepped outside.

233

The waitress came back for our meal orders, tucking loose hair behind her ears as she read off the list of specials.

"…and chunky crab chowder. That comes with a side salad, too."

We both nodded and Madison proceeded to point to a spot on her menu, asking what came with a particular dish. I realized then that I hadn't so much as glanced at the menu, but before I had the chance to panic, the waitress had already scribbled down Maddie's order, and her eyes were on me.

"What can I get you?"

What can I get you. Five words. Five

syllables. Simple. Any other person could have come up with a response bearing similar simplicity. Any other person could have either calculated the longing of their own taste buds and come up with an order or at least stuck their pointer finger to a spot on the list and faked it. The second I could have done.

"I…" I stammered, my vision dashing over the numerous options.

Ordering didn't scare me. Speaking to the waitress at Sand Creek didn't scare me. Having a plate of food in front of me didn't scare me. Even eating some of it didn't scare me. But the world stopped turning when I was asked what I wanted.

"Um, I'll have…uh…"

"She'll have the same, thanks." Madison said, handing back her menu.

The waitress furrowed her brow a little, perplexed, but nonetheless looked back down at the little pad of paper in her hands and quickly ran her pen along the lines before she made her way back to the kitchen.

"Sorry," I mumbled, looking down at my lap.

"For what?"

I glanced up at Maddie, who was taking a

sip from her glass with a nonchalant expression on her face.

"For…"

"Faith," she said, setting the glass down on the table. "Don't ever apologize for needing help, and don't ever be afraid to ask for it. Especially with me."

I didn't know what to say, so I remained silent while she continued.

"I didn't come here because I missed The Grove. I didn't come because I liked being reminded of, you know."

I bit my lip and shot a look out the window.

Beside us, people rushed along the sidewalks. Small children chased after each other, dripping popsicles in hand, speeding through the moments that wove to form their youth.

"I came here because you needed me, Faith."

"That's not all," I finally said. "I'm not the only reason."

It was as abrupt and stern as I had been in a long time, and I could tell that it caught Madison by surprise, too.

"You're right," she replied softly, "I came because I needed you, too."

238

Dear Todd,

I'm not the person I was before.

~Faith

Chapter Seventeen

I ate almost all of it.

Eating had never been the issue. It was that feeling I got after I ate, that feeling that I'd filled something. The guilt I had from being filled. Usually, I yearned to be empty immediately after I ate, or was forced to eat, anything. But not that day. That day, eating and talking and remembering made me feel like I was filling in cracks.

I suggested that we walk around after lunch, and Madison obliged. Outside, the sky had darkened with the arrival of an army of fluffy gray clouds. Less people occupied the streets as most had shuffled into restaurants and shops just as the thunder began to bellow from the distance. I knew that this could get in the way of getting where I wanted us to go, but that hardly diminished my relief over the fact that I probably wouldn't have to encounter anyone familiar along the way.

"Which way?" Madison would ask every time we came upon a crossroad. She seemed to like letting me lead the way, though I was sure she didn't know I had any specific location in mind. I'm not sure how she would have reacted had she known our destination.

241

Before I knew it, we were there.

The grass that painted the floor of the graveyard was speckled in the moisture that began to plummet from the sky. Droplets of rain ran off the stones before us, racing over the smooth, granite surfaces as if driven by an unknown fear and a longing to find sanctity in the grassy earth below. Madison hesitated at the entrance, a black gate accented in gold. The yard was small and located on the border of town, across the street from the oldest church in The Grove. I opened the gate and silently stepped inside. It was small, usually reserved for the most successful and elite deceased in town. There was one exception to the exclusion, but I didn't know where it was buried.

I turned around to face Maddie. Her eyes ran slowly over the yard, capturing the fine details of the space around her as though she was taking a photograph in her mind. She then looked back at me, opening her mouth to say something. Nothing was said, though. Nothing needed to be. She knew what I was silently asking, and answered with a motion of her hand in the direction of the far right of the yard.

I began to move in the same direction, my sandals sinking slightly into the soggy ground as I stepped. The rain began to pick up. I held out my palm so that the beads of liquid would accumulate on the skin of my hand. I could hear Madison walking gradually behind me, taking enough time to let me get ahead.

William Mulligan, 1920-1998

Cynthia Taft, 1931-2004

Rest in peace.

Beloved mother,

Brother,

Uncle,

Wife,

Son.

There was lightning in the distance. A flash of white erupted from behind the old church, filling the world around us in light for a split second.

"Faith," Maddie called from behind me.

I feared that she would tell me we should go back because of the storm, so I ignored her and continued to walk forward, scouring the site for his name.

"Faith," she repeated, and this time a hand fell onto my shoulder as she did.

I turned to face her.

"He's over there." she said softly, pointing toward a medium-sized stone four or five feet from where we stood.

I looked back at her face, which was stained in what appeared to be a mixture of tears and raindrops.

"Thanks," I said, and she nodded.

Todd Maguire.

There were a thousand things I could have said to Todd. A thousand things that could have begun to express my guilt, the frustration I had toward myself for letting him down. A thousand things. I had them written. They were all in a stack of notebooks in a box beneath my bed. All the things I had always wanted to say.

"Todd, I'm sorry I didn't come here sooner."

He was there. I could see him kneeling on the other side of the stone. He had on the red knit t-shirt he'd worn on our first date, one that could only still fit in an imaginary depiction of him. His eyes were wide and compassionate as he listened to me.

"I guess I could say I'm sorry for a lot of things, but I won't." I leaned my head back a little and attempted to blink away the accumulation of moisture in my eyes before I continued.

"I won't because I'm not here to be sorry. I'm here because I miss you, Todd. I miss the way you'd tilt your head to the side when someone said something you didn't understand. I miss the way you'd make me laugh so loud I thought I'd never breathe again." I smiled a little. "I miss the way you always treated people like everything about them made them amazing and beautiful. And for so long..."

A bolt of lightning lit the sky above the church. I jumped a little, noticing at that moment just how quickly my heart was beating.

"...for so long, I blamed myself. I told myself that I was the reason you couldn't be here to do any of that. But I'm not."

I took a shaky breath and tears began to cascade down my cheeks. The rain remained relentless, soaring toward the ground in thick droplets.

"I never thought I'd forgive myself for being so hard on you before you left. I never thought I'd forgive myself for pushing you over the edge. But while I was so busy being angry at myself, I never gave myself a chance to be mad at you. You left, Todd."

I took a glance behind my shoulder. Madison was at a far enough distance that she couldn't have heard what I said.

"You left and let me think that it was all my fault."

Thunder. Rain pounding the pavement.

"But I forgive you for that. Right here and now, I forgive you."

A parade of ducklings wobbled closely behind their mother across the road, moving in the direction of a small lake located a block behind the church. They ruffled their delicate white wings and remained close to one another as the rain tumbled over their little frames.

His eyes remained fixed on me, and he placed a hand on the stone between us. I smiled between sobs and laid my own hand on the other side of the stone.

"I know you'll always be here," I whispered, looking up at the church across the road and digging into my pocket to pull out a small paper bag. From the bag I drew a necklace from which three names dangled: *Madison, Todd, Faith.* "And I'm okay with that."

* * *

"There's just one more thing I have to do."

Madison tilted her head back to face the sky.

The rain had let up, but the sky remained glazed in gray. There was hesitance in her eyes, and her expression wordlessly asked me to call it a day.

"Please," I continued, "I promise it won't take long."

We came to a negotiation after a short while; we'd go wherever I needed to as long as Scott could drive us there, in case the storm picked up again. I was averse to the plan when she first suggested it, but it didn't take long for me to push my reluctance aside while I still had the nerve to do what had to be done.

Scott showed up ten minutes after I called,

giving Madison the chance to stand at a preferred

distance from Todd's grave. She didn't say

anything, though. Just stood and stared and looked

like she was about to crumble.

"Where to?" Scott asked as we piled into his

truck.

I situated myself in the middle between the

two of them.

"Home, first. I have to get something."

The rain picked up again, barreling down the

air in the form of thick, round droplets. Strands of

lightning tumbled down the space above the open

road and dashed back behind the clouds as quickly

as they had arrived. Scott opened his window and Maddie proceeded to do the same so that the sound of the nearing ocean's crashing waves and the rolling thunder could be heard as they argued in loud, low-toned voices. Crisp green leaves were torn from the trees on which they once resided and danced to the rhythm of the wind.

*   *   *

The weather hadn't let up by the time we got to the beach. Scott pulled up beside the boardwalk and grabbed the navy blue umbrella he'd stored beneath his seat for emergencies, reaching to hand it to me.

"No, thanks," I said, clutching the red and white shoebox firmly in my hands, "you two should take it."

Madison and Scott exchanged a quick look before we got out of the car.

I was instantly drenched in rainwater upon stepping out into the storm. We walked up the steps to the boardwalk and crossed over the side closest to the water.

"I think I should go it alone from here." I

said, turning to face the two of them, who huddled close beneath the shelter of the little umbrella.

Another exchanged glance.

"I'm not so sure that's a good idea, Faith." Scott said, his voice raising slightly so that he could be heard over the sound of the cascading of the rain on the boards beneath our feet and the rolling of waves on the nearby shore.

Madison looked up at Scott and said something at a volume too low for me to hear, then released her grip on the umbrellas pole and walked toward me.

"What's in the box, Faith?" she said quietly.

By her expression I could tell that she was concerned. Quite frankly, I couldn't blame her. I had asked to come out to the beach in the midst of a horrific thunderstorm with a soggy little shoebox and thin explanation. I opened my mouth to expound every last detail of the contents of my box, but decided instead to let her see for herself. I handed her the box. She reached to open it, looking up at me at the same time so that I may reassure her that she had permission to do so.

I don't know what she read in the first letter she drew from my collection. I don't know what I'd felt or wanted to say when I wrote it, but that didn't

257

really matter. As her eyes chewed the words and swallowed the sentences, tears began to stream down her cheeks. It was at that moment that I realized he was hers, too. Todd was not some glorious little secret I could keep in a box beside my bed. For every childhood memory and perfect moment of blissful youth, Maddie was there.

I opened my mouth to ask that she come with me, but she was already swiveling back around to face Scott. She had placed the letter she read back on top of the pile and now ran back to stand beneath the umbrella.

"Go ahead," she called out over the roar of

the enraged storm.

In her eyes I could see that she understood. Before I could begin to apologize for having ever lost sight of the affect the loss of Todd had on her, my feet were patting against the soggy dark beige sand in the direction of the water.

And I ran.

I ran as though the world was prepping to burst behind my back, though many a time I'd felt like it already had. When I came to the water, my initial instinct was to take the first letter and throw it out to sea. The wind made this impossible, its gusts pushing inland. I looked back and noticed that Scott and Maddie were nowhere to be seen, as they had probably taken a seat on one of the boardwalk's benches. This made my new plan far more possible to follow through with.

The water was colder than I had anticipated. It rolled over my toes and stung the bottom of my feet. The box in my hands sat limp, its edges soft and moist as the cardboard slowly deteriorated beneath the weight of the heavy rain. I began to pace quickly toward the water until I found myself waist-deep. The first wave to come down on me had inconceivable force, knocking me off my feet. I held the box to my chest with one hand and used the

260

other to push back the water and come up for air.

I knew right then and there that I could die.

As soon as I was back up, the next wave barreled along the shore, tall enough to send me tumbling back again. After I came up once again, I could see that there was little time before the next came. I opened the box, the top of which stuck to it with the moist cardboard as an adhesive to itself, and began to tear out the letters. They held to each other, pasted in water, so many went to sea as a pair. I lifted the first letters, balled them in my hand, and threw them in the direction of the foggy horizon. The rest I left to drift in the waves which still battled with my balance as I watched the shards

of a life once reluctantly embraced float off every

which way.

They were free.

Dear Todd,

My tutor read me a poem today about a room full of butterflies, all dancing on air dressed in vibrant satin wings. It was written by a young girl who was dying of cancer. This was one of the many empathy exercises that have been snuck into my lessons to help with my depression- surely the result of one of the many meetings that have been held between my parents and doctors and therapists and teachers and so forth. The poem was about how she'd fly with the butterflies when she died. I was

263

supposed to write about how it must have felt for

such a young girl to already be coming up with

fantasies about Heaven, life after life. It was hard

because I couldn't stop thinking about those

butterflies. I wondered if we were allowed to fly

with them even if we left on our own terms, like you

did. I hope I dream of them tonight. Maybe if we fly

together long enough, I won't have to wake up.

"I'll recline on the hum of a passing breeze,

traveling listlessly above the roar of the unkind

world beneath my uncharted tracks."

~Faith

Chapter Eighteen

The clouds didn't disappear from the solid gray sky. The wind didn't slow its pace to that of a soft breeze. The rain didn't let up.

But as I dragged myself toward higher sands beneath the weight of my sopping wet clothes with empty hands and a fuller heart, it became incredibly clear that I didn't need any of that. My storm was calmed.

Madison and Scott sat on a green bench in front of the boardwalk railing. I realized upon walking up the steps and catching sight of them that they could not have witnessed my previous actions from behind the reed-covered sand dune in front of them. I decided then that telling them that I'd been crazy enough to submit myself to the merciless waters was unnecessary.

"Faith," Madison turned her head toward me and waved.

There was a semblance of peacefulness and ease painted across her face as she smiled and flagged me toward their spot on the bench. I didn't question what such an expression could have been a result of. Sometimes you're just better off taking happiness for what it is. In this case, it was real.

I quickened my pace and came beside them, leaning forward so that my drenched head found shelter beneath their umbrella. The thunder had ceased, shifting the ears of those who still roamed the outside world to the scream of the wind that tumbled over the streets and danced across the sidewalks.

"How do you feel?" Madison asked as the three of us lingered in the heart of the storm.

"Great," I said, smiling as if the world had never before seen a brighter day, "I feel great."

We sat in the car for a short while, just watching the rain. I bit my tongue to keep from chattering my teeth, afraid that Scott or Madison would notice and be concerned. I didn't want them to worry about me. I didn't want anyone to worry about me.

Beep, beep. Scott's phone sounded from his glove compartment.

"Would you grab that for me? It's probably Mom."

Madison opened the compartment and I reached in for the phone, fumbling through a mess of folded papers and old gum wrappers before my fingers came across the slim cell phone. I handed him the phone.

"Hello?" he said, pressing it against his ear as he leaned against the steering wheel.

"I'll have to see…yeah, I know. Okay, well, I'll see if I can make it. Yeah, thanks for letting me know. I'll talk to you later. Seeya."

Scott closed the phone and slipped it into his pocket.

"What was that about?" I asked softly.

Chills ran up and down my spine as a reminder of the harsh cold waters that had nearly swallowed me only a short time ago.

"It was Dylan," he said, referring to a friend of his I'd met two or three times before. "They're

269

having a bonfire tomorrow night, he wanted me to go."

A silence fell over the car. But at that descending of my heart into the shadows of the painful memory, something emerged. A strength, or a longing to be strong.

"We should go."

There were many times I'd felt like I was throwing Madison for a loop since she'd returned to The Grove. This time had the most impact on both of us, though. Because this time, the audience to my words and actions was not the only party to be surprised by my plot twists.

"I mean, if you wouldn't mind," I continued, turning then to face Madison, "and if you want to."

Before the two could speak, the world froze. I smiled and basked in the still moment for as long as it lasted, appreciating its timing and loving the opportunity I was given to feel as if ridding the weight of the world from my shoulders was as simple as giving it a little lift.

Madison's face was immediately a reflection of the concern I would have predicted she'd express had I put more than a moment's thought into the whole thing. Scott's reaction was far less predictable.

"Yeah," he said, wrapping an arm over my shoulder and pulling me in for a small bear hug the way he had when we were younger and things were simpler. "Yeah, that sounds good."

I watched my ceiling for nearly three hours that night in bed. Thoughts meandered through my head and walked back out with the coming of new thoughts. None really held much significance, but I didn't mind that. It's the trivial, random thoughts that let the mind rest.

There was worry, of course. But that wasn't difficult to replace with the longing to see the way they'd all look at me when my greatest battle was fought. No more expressions of pity. No more careful words and tones. Going to the bonfire would prove the newfound strength my mom had doubted.

To a greater extent, it would prove to me the existence of the strength that I had long since lost hope in gaining. Things were better, I was better. These things I knew with certainty as I put to ease my heavy eyelids and submerged myself in my subconscious, the former prison that had become my refuge.

Dear Todd,

We've all thought about it, that I'm sure of. But I don't think I can recall a single occasion on which someone addressed it out loud. And as many letters as I've written, it would seem that even I have failed to ask.

Why?

Why did you leave?

But I guess, when I think about it, it's almost a silly question. We all saw it. We all saw the pain you were in, but none of us chose to look closer. None of

274

us chose to do anything about it. None of us chose

to accept your reality, because we were all too busy

admiring the painting you chose to portray, the

colors you chose to let us see. You put on such a

show, Todd. Our only fault was that we stayed in

our seats.

~Faith

Chapter Nineteen

That day went by painfully slow. Mom and Dad had left for work by the time I was awake. Scott was down in the kitchen frying up some eggs on the stove to the beat of the classic rock playing on the living room stereo.

"You hungry?" he asked, holding his arm against his mouth in a yawn as I sauntered in drowsily.

I paused to stop myself from denying the offer.

"Sure." I said plainly. "Two eggs.

Scrambled, if you don't mind."

Scott looked back with a smile and shook his head.

"She really has made a difference." he said softly, easing a large yellow omelet from the pan to his plate.

I took a seat at the table and reached for the carton of orange juice that had been left beside the vase of daises in the center. Outside, I could hear Stacy Camden's boyfriend's engine revving as he sat atop his gleaming black motorcycle by the curb in front of the neighbor's driveway. He was the kind of guy that turned heads in a place like The Grove, and as Stacy pranced down her lawn in a skimpy pair of ripped denim shorts and a semi-see-through tank top, I figured that was what she liked about him. Todd once said that the only thing we teenagers should rebel against is ourselves. I don't think I understood what he meant until that moment.

"What?" I said, realizing then that I had missed what Scott said.

"Madison. She has really helped since she's been here."

"Oh, yeah. Grab me a glass?"

Scott went into the cabinet and took out two

glasses, then walked over and set them both down on the table. I uncapped the carton and poured into them.

"Not that you couldn't have done it on your own. We both know that's not true." he smiled.

I smiled back weakly, my eyes steady on the glass in my hands.

"Right?" he said, tilting his head in attempt to catch my gaze.

"What? Yeah." I said, looking up to give another smile for the sake of reassuring him.

He turned back and went toward the stove, his expression appearing seemingly satisfied.

"What difference would it make, anyway?" I said, taking a small sip of my juice. "Either way, I'm better."

Scott ran his spatula along the bottom of the pan, moving around my eggs, and shrugged.

"Hey, would you mind if I went for a jog with some guys? Like, after we eat. I mean, would you be okay…here. Without me…"

"Of course." I responded quickly.

He took a peek back at me and again shook his head, a small smile resting on his face.

After Scott left, there wasn't much for me to do. The house was spotless after the prior day's visit from our cleaning lady, leaving me without a floor

to vacuum or a load of laundry to do, both of which

had become fairly customary for me ever since I'd

stopped going to school. School. Sometimes I

wondered what they said about me after I was gone.

All lies, I was sure. The truth is hardly a common

facet of adolescent storytelling, especially on the

Jersey Shore, where interesting, conversation-

inducing news was never particularly abundant. I

thought about going upstairs to write a letter to

Todd before I remembered the empty space beneath

my bed where a little cardboard shoe-box once sat.

I meandered up to Mom and Dad's room to

see if there were any good books on their bedside tables, only to discover that Mom had finally convinced Dad to join book club, judging by the two dog-eared copies of Sylvia Plath's *The Bell Jar*. It was one I'd read at least three or four times before. I hopped up on the bed and opened to a random page of the book, running my eyes over the text and becoming familiar once again with the material.

Minutes passed in a matter of hours. I quickly grew bored with the book and laid down in the hope that I'd fall asleep and wake up right before it was time to leave. This was, of course, as far-fetched a dream as can be, and I knew it. But something had me thinking that, with the right attitude, I just might be able to put my mind at ease for as long as it would take to enter my subconscious. I took a breath, relaxed the muscles in my arms, and slept.

Part Three

Chapter Twenty

Madison

The air smelled of burning wood and salty seawater. As we unloaded ourselves from the car and stepped out onto the pavement, I could see that the row of cars parked beside us extended all the way across The Grove's beach and crossed over the border into the next town over. We had been lucky enough to obtain a spot in front of the pavilion, which was only a short walk from where the bonfires usually took place. I had nearly walked over to the beach myself with the intention of meeting up with Scott and Faith, seeing as it was only across the street from my house, until Scott called on his way home and asked if he could pick me up before he stopped at his house to get Faith.

"Has Faith called you at all today?"

I furrowed my brow. "No, I don't think so."

There was a pause in conversation as something beneath the hood of the truck began to rumble lightly. We both drew in a breath and in his eyes I could see him silently praying for the life of Ilma, who he had come around to naming on a

287

spontaneous car ride to nowhere he'd taken me on

the day before last. The rumbling quieted to a low

mumble and soon stopped, evoking a sigh from my

mouth and a "Thank God!" from Scott's. We both

laughed.

"Did she call you?" I asked.

"What? Oh, no. That's what was strange.

I'm not really allowed to leave her home alone, at

least not for a long time. When I do, it's usually just

for a five minute drive up the road to grab a pizza

or something."

"What about when you're away at school?"

We passed their street and continued down

288

Ocean Avenue.

"My parents try to work their schedules around her." he shrugged.

"That's rough."

"Yeah. But see, usually when I make a quick stop down the street or whatever, I'll get at least three or four calls asking where I am, when I'll get back. I used to think she was afraid something would happen to me while I was gone, until one day when I had to pick up some milk for breakfast last summer. She called in tears, saying something about how she couldn't be alone with her thoughts. It was like she was terrified of herself and what she

might... do to herself without anyone around to stop her."

I bit my bottom lip and watched as we passed the tourist-attracting storefronts and restaurants that were abundant in the area we found ourselves in. Distractions had become my guilt-coping method.

"I mean, I'm not afraid that she isn't okay right now or anything like that," he continued, "I called her up on my way back to make sure that she was, and she sounded fine. It's just... "

"Different." I finished for him. "You're just used to her being more dependant. She's changed."

Scott turned onto a street beside a small pizzeria and made another turn onto a side street back in the direction of their house.

"It's not that I'm not glad she has," he said, slowly stopping the car to wait for a row of geese to cross the street, "I love how happy she is. But…what about when you leave?"

The geese had all crossed by then, but Scott sat still in the road, his eyes on the wheel.

"What do you mean?" I said, turning around to make sure there weren't any cars waiting behind us. There weren't.

"Come on, Madison. You know you won't be

here to keep her company forever. What about when

you go back to the city, what happens then? Even if

you stayed the rest of the summer, there's still

college."

Scott and I had talked about me extending

my visit multiple times, and by that point I had even

brought it up to Mom, who was no less than

absolutely overjoyed at the thought of me staying

the whole summer. I had even added to the list of

places I'd go with Faith, finding that at least one

came to mind nearly every time I traveled in and

around town. As for college, the thought of that had

taken back seat to my thoughts of The Grove, and

the people in it.

"Faith doesn't need me." I said, repeating the words over and over in my head in attempt to fully convince myself that they could be true.

Scott looked at me as if I had told a bad joke.

What remained of the car ride was silent until we pulled up beside the Anderson driveway.

"You ready?" he asked as Faith bounded down the pavement in a baggy yellow tank top and loose denim shorts.

"As I'll ever be."

The sun was low on the horizon now, its light giving the earth around us one last kiss before it retreated back into its home in the unknown. The air we breathed in was thick and humid, leaving a sticky taste on the inside of my cheeks. I wondered then, for the first time, what my dad was doing at that moment. I could see him sitting hunched over the coffee table in our spacious apartment with a plate of steamed vegetables and won-tons, tie-loosened as his eyes danced over the reel of unfortunate headlines on the 9 o'clock news. And Miss Maguire, what of her? Was she lounging on her couch in the heart of a house teeming with hanging photographic depictions of the people who once made the life she had known before misery struck? I hoped she wasn't alone. I hoped my dad wasn't alone, too. But I knew they were. It's a funny thing, money is. Rich people on reality shows and in movies are never lonely. No, they always have the company of their many friends and lovers and private-jet fliers and champagne servers. They don't ache past the point of a tear shed with the loss of a new handbag or the break in a two-month-old friendship. They don't sit at empty dinner tables with bloodshot eyes and somber expressions, because they're rich, so they must have people to share their lives with. They're rich, so they must be smiling.

The three of us walked down the boardwalk toward the screaming and laughter that boomed from the other end of the beach. Faith seemed nervously excited, and I wondered just what it was that she was anticipating. When we were little, we always thought the big kids who got to go to bonfires and get in disputes over trivial little issues were the coolest beings in the universe, their lives were just *so* interesting.

"How many people do you think are there already?" Faith asked. "How many do you think

296

will be there?"

I looked at Scott, who I was sure had a far more accurate guess at the answer than I could possibly have.

"Hard to say," he said, glancing down at the phone in his hand. "Depends on how many show up."

He smiled.

Faith rolled her eyes.

"There was a beach party down in Witherford earlier, so there might be more than usual. The underclassmen high school guys love trying to pick up benny girls from those things, so they'll probably bring a bunch of them."

"Ugh," Faith and I said in unison.

We looked at each other and exchanged a laugh. Teen girls who came down from New York over the summer often had a greater taste for alcohol than for the shore itself, and for that reason they usually ended adolescent Grove festivities early after getting caught sneaking in kegs and wine coolers. The majority of kids from The Grove were surprisingly lacking in an interest in drugs and alcohol, with the exception of the few who chose to partake in such things with friends from other towns. This only heightened the friction between sober residents and party-craving tourists, most of whom journeyed to our shore blinded by the expectations conceived by the media's portrayal of our culture.

We made our way around the bend to the ramp that descended onto the beach.

"Scott!" a voice called from behind us.

The three of us turned to face a pair of blonde girls bounding toward Scott.

"Hey, I didn't know you two were coming," Scott said, smiling at them as they came to a halt behind Faith.

"Wouldn't miss it," one said, flipping back

her hair.

"Is this your…" the other began to ask, motioning to Faith.

"This is my sister, Faith." Scott finished for her.

Faith seemed terribly uncomfortable I momentarily feared that she might leave right then and there. Instead, she stuck out her hand, looked both girls in the eye, and smiled.

"Nice to meet you," the second girl said, making a face at Faith's hand and pausing before shaking it, confused by the formal gesture.

I looked at Scott and watched as his eyes

followed the two hands as they joined and scrutinized the act with extreme focus, as though averting his sight for so much as a moment would result in the disappearance of the normality occurring before him. Faith was being Faith.

My emotions spun wildly as we trekked down the ramp onto the beach, each footstep bringing us that much closer to the unknown.

Dear Todd,

I should be done writing you by now. The concept of doing so in the first place was for me to make peace with you, with what happened. I don't know if it has worked. Whether or not it has, the time has come for me to stop. I know I've made such a statement more than once before in past letters, but this time I mean it. I need to let you go. Madison is taking me out to lunch tomorrow. I haven't told her, but afterwards I'd like to visit the spot where they buried you. Madison doesn't drive, for some reason. She can, she just doesn't. If I could drive,

I'd ask Scott if I could borrow his truck. Then I'd go way down south and find an empty road in the middle of nowhere, with a rocky horizon full of mountains. And I'd sit in the bed of that truck and watch the sky for hours, listening only to the soft song of an unheard nature. Anyway, after we visit your grave, I want to get rid of these letters. I haven't decided how just yet, but that's what I want to do. It's time to move on.

~Faith

Chapter Twenty-One

Faith

It was like discovering a different dimension. We stepped out onto the sand and found ourselves in a skewed version of the past, as though someone had taken a written copy of the life we once knew and marked it up in red ink, crossing out names and making corrections. In this revised adaptation of our lives, there was music. Music that people moved to, danced to and swung to. Music that silenced our doubt and left only enough room in the summer night's air for something we couldn't see or touch or even think about. Something that connected even those who had for so long chosen in favor of self-ostracism. And that something radiated from the flames around which we danced and waged war with the moon, who grew jealous of the glow.

The world was bright, so we basked in it. The music was loud, so we danced in it. There was nothing to keep me from indulging in the atmosphere. Nothing, but you.

Scott and Madison and I danced to the beat of some cheesy techno song, the two of them occasionally stealing glances at me with half-worried expressions. I had to show them there was nothing to fear. I was fine. I was wonderful. I was part of this world and a member of these people. I could feel some of the many attendees staring at me. They knew who I was. I was Todd Maguire's girlfriend, a sophomore in high school. Holder of three community service awards and vice president of the sophomore class. I was the girl they wanted to be friends with, because I knew the right things to say and I looked right and acted right. Everything about me and my existence was right. And you'd be there any minute to kiss my forehead and point up

306

at the stars, all nestled in their pretty blue blanket at a safe distance from where we stood. And you'd tell me how special I was, how wonderful I made you feel. You'd tell me how much you cared about me. Then after a little while your expression would fade and you'd say something else, but this time it wasn't something I wanted to hear. It wasn't, so I'd laugh and pretend that it was just a joke. For all I knew it could have been, until the day you told the punch line and we all stopped laughing.

I could feel the anxiety Madison took on every time another head turned. I tried to ignore it. Couldn't she see that everything was perfect? Our former classmates sat cross-legged drinking from oversized cans of iced tea. They danced in tie-dyed sweatshirts and joked until every bellow of laughter melted into one continuous beat, keeping time with the music in our ears and in our chests.

We were perfect.

This life was perfect.

Something called my name, or rather whispered it from a close enough distance. The sound penetrated the wall that bliss had built me and made me turn my head.

Faith.

I scanned the space around us, visually

scavenging for the caller.

Faith.

I swiveled around countless times, chasing the directions from which the voice sounded.

"Faith?"

I turned to face Madison, whose face was drenched in worry at the sight of my turning and scanning. It was the face my mom had given me on the way home from the hospital as I poked and prodded at the bandages on my wrists. It was the face Scott gave me when he came home and found me crying at the bottom of the stairs that day he got stuck in traffic and came home from the grocery store a few minutes late. It was the face I had worked so hard to get rid of. And it was back.

I stretched the corners of my mouth upward and asked her what was wrong. She hesitated, watching me closely with that face.

"Nothing," she lied, "it's nothing."

The night progressed for minutes. Minutes collided with hours and so on until the sky was black and painted in stars and the clock was well into double-digits. We spent most of that time dancing and sitting in the sand and avoiding the eyes of those who saw but were too cautious to approach. A few people greeted Madison, offering one-armed hugs and exchanging casual

conversation. They didn't say anything to me, but

that was okay. Everything was okay.

There were four or five coolers beside the

boardwalk, all completely stocked up with sodas

and iced teas. Madison and I got up from where

we'd been sitting on a striped blanket with some of

Scott's friends to retrieve a few cans. We

maneuvered through a maze of couples and pow-

wows of friends and guys playing guitars, our feet

tapping the few bare spaces left on the sand. The

coolers were blue and coated in a layer of moisture.

As Madison bent down to pull out our drinks, I

turned around to face the fire in the distance.

That was when I saw him.

The flames that previously inhabited the
ground on which he stood had vanished, leaving
only a light dusting of ashes around his feet. He
stood with his back straight and his chin up. He was
laughing. Smiling and holding his hands in his
pockets the way he did when someone said
something that made him blush. He was there, and
he was beautiful. For a moment, I was comforted by
the illusion. But only a moment.

The flames rose back up from the ground as
quickly as they had previously disappeared,

swallowing Todd. And as they did, his expression remained constant, as though the smile was a permanent fixture on his imaginary face.

"*No!*" I screamed in horror.

Dear Todd,

I love you.

~Faith

Chapter Twenty-Two

Madison

The scream strangled the roar of the crowd, choking it until one by one, we were all silent.

"I'm so sorry," Faith turned to face me, tears cascading down her flushed cheeks, "but I've got to go."

She pushed passed me, stepping around the coolers, and fled to the boardwalk. I followed behind quickly, continually reaching for and missing her shoulder.

"Faith!" I called as her pace intensified,

sending her in a sprint up the worn wooden steps of

the boardwalk.

I could feel everyone's eyes on our backs. If

they hadn't been watching us before, they certainly

made up for it then. I looked back, scanning the

crowd until my own eyes caught sight of Scott, who

was racing toward me.

"What's going on?" he asked, frantic.

"Where's Faith?"

"I…" my head throbbed as I attempted to

spill the words that could begin to explain exactly

what had just occurred. "She…Faith…."

316

I pointed to the steps. In that moment, the gears in my head shifted backwards, reminding me of the time Faith, Todd and I had once played manhunt as little kids. Faith had taken a hiding place beneath the shadow of Todd's house, where she sat and stared at the sky for nearly half an hour. We had all given up on finding her when she finally came out. She had a small smile stretching across her face when she told us that she had been in plain sight all along.

Scott and I moved quickly toward the stairs. At the top, Faith was still nowhere to be found.

"Where do you think she went?" Scott

asked, his voice straining for strength to cover the
weak, uneasy tone beneath it.

"Home, maybe? I don't know." I replied
helplessly.

"I'll get the truck." he said, reaching into his
pocket for his keys.

"Don't come back for me. Go straight home,
you'll get there quicker. Call me if she's there. I'll
walk."

Scott hesitated, then nodded and ran back
down the boardwalk in the direction of the pavilion.
I waited until he was nearly out of sight, unsure of
where to turn, what to do. I walked down the steps

to the sidewalk, counting the visible cracks in the wood beneath my feet and wondering for what may have been the first time how it could hold up for so long beneath the weight of the many who tread on it every day. The cracks were nothing but small indications that the structure's endurance was not eternal. They were little reminders that our old boardwalk, solid and strong as it may be, could someday collapse and retire its duty with the blink of an eye.

"Faith?" I called.

No response.

I listened closely to the world around the

space in which I stood, silently waiting for whatever came next. There was no way to know for sure if Faith was where I suspected she was, no way except to see for myself.

As I walked toward the middle of town, I pulled from my pocket the letter she had shown me the day she threw her box out to sea.

...this is where I like to write. It's where I've written most of my letters to you, and I think it might be the most magical place in the world.

...yes, that's where it is. You'd love it, Todd. It's between all the madness and movement of this world. It's like a point of recollection, a spot where

you don't have to say or do, but only be. It's where I

feel safe.

The letter was almost lost in the storm, as it had slipped out from beneath the cover of the box as she ran toward the beach that day. Had it not passed my feet as I made my way back toward Scott, it's fair to say we'd have never seen it again. For one reason or another, I didn't give it back. Maybe because it was beautiful and lifted some of the weight from the tattered folded paper that already resided in my pocket. Maybe because I didn't want to feel like we were letting every piece of him go.

* * *

"Faith."

I crouched down beside the fence, listening to her muffled sobs, then made my way toward the end of the fence. The air had become chill by then, and the only sound to break the even silence was the slow, somber chirp of a single cricket. The space between the two fences was narrow, just wide enough for me to go through without standing sideways. I kept my eyes on the ground in fear that I might accidentally step on Faith without the aid of any light brighter than the closest streetlight, which was fairly dim to begin with.

"Madison?"

"Yeah, it's me, Faith. Where are you?"

"You should go, Madison. Just leave me here."

Her voice came from only a few feet away, so I stopped and stood where I was, scanning the ground to catch sight of her.

"Come on, Faith. Lets go home."

"I'm not going anywhere. Just leave, Madison," her tone quickly grew hostile. "Just leave me here to die. I should never have gone tonight, you shouldn't have made me go, Madison. How could you make me go?"

323

All her life, the only person Faith saw fit to blame for anything was herself. Her words sliced the night-air and stung in my chest.

"Faith," I reached down to feel for her, biting my tongue to keep from erupting in argument, "lets just go, please? We were really worried about you. Scott has probably already called your mom. Come on, Faith. Faith?"

There was a moment of silence. The cricket sang much lower now, as though he was secretly eavesdropping on us from the safety of his grass bed.

Finally, Faith stood. Her face came up

beneath the inkling of light that shone from the streetlight to reveal a collage of tear streaks and a pair of blood-shot eyes. I reached out to take her hand and she held it back, looking down at her feet. I turned around and started back slowly, listening closely to the sound of her footsteps to be sure that she was following behind.

We came out of the fence silently and almost automatically started back en route to Fraigle Street.

My phone rang a minute or two into our walk. It was Scott checking to see if I'd found Faith. I felt immediately guilty for not having thought to call him as soon as I found her, but his voice reassured me that while the situation was incredibly stressful and frightening, it wasn't the first time something like it had happened. When I got off the phone, Faith was staring at me.

"You really scared everyone." I said, my eyes taking turns keeping watch over my feet and the road ahead to avoid making contact with hers. "Your parents came home early. Scott called and told them you were missing…they were worried sick about you, Faith. They almost called the cops."

"Uh-huh," she mumbled.

I stopped, jarred by her response.

"Uh-huh? That's the best you could do? This isn't like you, Faith."

"And how would you know?" she snapped, lifting her head so that her eyes made full contact with mine. "You left. You weren't here, Madison. While you were living it up in the city with your new friends in your new life, some of us were left here. Some of us were left to pick up the pieces you so easily left behind."

She was yelling now, her tone harsh and biting. It stirred something within me, urging me to fight back. I resisted for a moment, monitoring the reel of comebacks that spiraled through my head.

But the word *easily* ignited a spark in me, making the spewing of my own words irresistible.

"You think it was *easy* to leave, Faith? You think it was easy to go after what happened? You think I didn't want to be there for you?"

Faith turned back around and continued in the direction we'd been walking in, her steps cold and hard on the pavement. But I remained still.

"You think what happened wasn't just as hard on me?" I screamed.

Faith stopped.

She slowly turned around to face me, her expression blank and condescending.

328

"Of course it wasn't." she said matter-of-factly. "I loved him, Madison."

Letter #184

Dear Todd,

Sometimes I wish we hadn't met. Other times, I wish I wouldn't wish for such horrible things.

~Faith

Chapter Twenty-Three

Faith

Truer words had yet to surpass my lips until that moment. It was the declaration of my pain and the justification of any pain I had done unto others. I loved him.

Madison stared at me, her face drained of its color. The part of me that wanted to apologize, to say that I knew how much he meant to her, too, had by then been stabbed by the longing to be recognized as the greatest bearer of the pain; the most cheated by our loss. Any consideration I might have had as to taking back my words had already been scalded with his image in the flames. I did not want to hurt Madison, but I needed her to know the superiority of my suffering.

As I stood and watched, she reached into her pocket, pulling out what appeared to be a folded piece of paper. We were standing a short distance away from each other now, so she took a few long, quiet steps toward me. By now, my face was saturated in tears. But not Madison's. Hers was dry.

"Read this." she said solemnly, handing me the paper.

My hand shook lightly as I reached for it and I prayed she wouldn't notice. I was strong. If she couldn't see it now, she never would.

"What is this?" I asked, running my fingers over the worn paper.

"Just read it." she said, nodding toward the paper, urging me to open it.

I gently opened the paper, taking great care out of fear that it might fall apart in my hands. It was wrinkled and torn as it had clearly been folded and refolded over time. The edges of the paper curled in a little, and when it was completely open I could see that the lines were faded and nearly invisible. But the words remained, dark and strong on the tattered page.

"Oh my God."

I looked up at Madison, who seemed to have lost her composure the moment my eyes were fed with the muddled, scratchy writing on the paper. Tears streamed in marathons down her cheeks. Her eyes were locked on the ground, where they seemed to be attempting to mask sorrow with contempt.

"Dear Madison," I said aloud.

My voice cracked the first time, breaking beneath the weight of the words it was forced to utter.

"Dear Madison," I repeated, "I am so sorry I have to do this."

I betrayed you, Faith. I don't deserve you.

"By the time you read this, I will already be gone. But before I leave, I have to apologize for everything, especially what happened the other night. I care about you so, so much, Madison. But it was wrong for me to…"

My voice cracked once again and I held a hand up to my mouth as I silently completed the sentence.

"…it was wrong for me to kiss you. It was wrong, because I knew that this was going to happen. I knew I was going to leave. Please,

whatever you do, don't blame yourself for that.

Don't ever blame yourself for my decision. I don't

know what else there is to say. Please show this

letter to Faith after I leave. Tell her it's not her fault,

either. You're better off. You're both better off."

I was sobbing by then, my tears diving onto

the paper and drowning the words.

"Todd Maguire."

Letter #244

Dear Todd,

Sometimes, the only thing that really helps me get by is knowing that what we had was almost worth having to use your name in the past-tense.

~Faith

Chapter Twenty-Four

Madison

The moon was set low in the evening sky that night, so much so that one might think it was anxious to escape the scene playing out beneath its light on our side of the planet. I glanced down either side of the sidewalk and checked the time on my phone once again. He should have been there by then, and I knew that if he didn't show up soon, Faith would get there before we had a chance to talk. I shivered a little at the thought of Faith. My feelings toward her had become so mixed; when she and I were together without Todd, I saw her as my best friend. But when he was around, she was no more than an obstacle. It's funny, when you don't want to like someone, not liking them becomes a pretty easy thing to do. You can find a thousand things wrong with them in a matter of seconds, and before you know it, that person has become your greatest aggravation, even after nearly a lifetime of friendship.

"Todd,"

His eyes paid me a moment's worth of attention before they reclaimed their position on the ground and occasionally up in the night sky.

"Hey," he said, stopping in front of me.

"Want to sit?" I sat down on the bench behind us, reaching behind my back quickly for a subtle smooth of my hair out of fear that the humidity was making it frizz.

"I'm good." he said.

I looked up at him, my expression searching. It was a few moments before he noticed, though, and by then I must have looked merely desperate for him to say something.

"Faith's coming, right?" I asked.

"Yeah."

"And you're going to…"

He nodded quickly, as if begging that I refrain from finishing the question. I nodded back.

"She'll be here soon," he said after a minute or two, "you should probably go."

Faith looked as though she was bursting from the inside out. I watched as her body curled in, leaning forward as if in search of support, of which there was none.

She ran down the street so quickly that, had I not known the circumstances, I would not have

341

guessed it was her, but rather someone driven by

sheer madness. I considered racing after her, but

knew that first I needed to speak to Todd. It took a

while to find him. I knew he was taking her down by

the water to break up with her, but somehow I

couldn't bring myself to believe he'd stay in that

spot after the fact. But sure enough, he was there.

He sat with his legs crossed and his face turned

upward toward the sky.

"Todd," I said, jogging in his direction and

taking a seat beside him on the sand. "I was looking

all over for you."

He said nothing.

"How did she take it?" I asked softly.

Todd looked out at the water, his straight expression unchanging.

"You should go, Madison."

I furrowed my brow.

"Todd?" I said, tilting my head for a better view of his face.

His eyes were glassy and looked as though they were on the verge of erupting in tears. I frowned sympathetically.

"I know how hard that must have been on you," I said, resting a hand on his shoulder.

Todd stood up, shrugging off the hand. I

stood, too.

"Todd?" I said as he began to walk away.
"Todd?"

The last one was a scream. I bellowed his name in the hope that it would shake his insides, reminding him that I was there, I existed. I was the girl he truly cared for. I was the one he wanted to be with. I was the girl he kissed, and the girl he was leaving his girlfriend for. But even then, I was still the one he left behind.

The guilt slammed me in the stomach as Faith crumpled the paper into a ball in her fist and quickly turned back in the direction of her house. I had always known I'd have to tell her eventually, but not like this. Betrayal hung stagnant in the air, reminding me of the truth that had for so long been stuffed in my pocket, hidden from a world that knew not of the wicked intentions I had tried so hard to leave behind.

Dear Todd,

*You used to love taking pictures. I remember when
we were young and your mom got you a dark blue
re-usable camera for Christmas. It was back before
digital photography was as typical as it is now, so I
remember going down to the drug store on Main
and getting pictures developed nearly every week.
Madison and I were your most common subjects,
and I bet if I went through the boxes we've stored
away in the attic of all my old things I could find at
least four or five stacks of pictures mainly
comprised of us sitting on the beach or riding our*

346

bikes or building forts out of snow. Those are the

memories you chose to capture, because those were

the things that made you happy. That little blue

camera showed its face each and every time there

was a smile on yours. And though I can so vividly

recall it being a seemingly permanent fixture

dangling from your wrist, I can't say I remember

the day you stopped using it. I don't think it broke,

but maybe it did.

~Faith

Chapter Twenty-Five

Faith

That was the day the world tore in half. The run home was exhausting, leaving me short of breath. Naturally, this only made me want to run faster. The streets were stripped of all inhabitants, leaving me to sob to the beat of the melody of silence. I slowed to a near stop before cutting the corner onto my street, attempting to maintain some level of unquestionable calm before I could escape to the sanctity of my bedroom, which seemed

348

worlds away as I closed the door behind me and waited for the click of the door to trigger the eruption of my universe. It wasn't the first time I'd slipped away for miniscule periods of time, though most went unnoticed as they took place late at night or extremely early in the morning. But something was different this time.

"Faith,"

The voice came from the kitchen. I walked toward it cautiously, stuffing the balled-up paper in my pocket.

"Scott," I sighed, slightly relieved that my first interaction after what had just taken place wouldn't be with my parents, "where are Mom and Dad?"

Scott sat at the kitchen table, his face in his hands. He looked up, his expression firm and cold. I quietly anticipated the usual; he would give me a short, slap-on-the-wrist lecture about how worried they were about me, followed by an expression of sympathy and an expressed hope that he wasn't being too hard on me. And when all was said and done, I could go up to my room and wait for all that I now knew to settle in. And I could abandon the horrendous numb feeling that had crept up on me on the run home and replace it with a long, vomit-inducing sob.

"I told them it was a misunderstanding," he said, his eyes fixed on the table, then on his hands, and back on the table. "I told them we hadn't heard you say you were going up to the beach club bathrooms, and that Madison had found you on your way back. They went back to their party."

I nodded, looking down at my feet, which I now noticed were throbbing after having traveled so quickly in the worst possible footwear, an old pair of flip-flops.

"Thank you," I said softly.

"Don't," he responded hastily, his tone

hostile, "don't thank me."

I was taken aback, baffled as to what I should say next. He eliminated that issue, though, when he began to speak again.

"Does the fact that we were all worried sick mean *anything* to you, Faith? Do you have any idea how awful it is wondering where you might be, what you might be doing? Has that crossed your mind any one of the times you've done something like this?"

I swallowed so hard that it felt as though my heart was in my throat, digging its way to the surface so that it may leap from my mouth and shatter on the floor.

"I can listen to this from Mom and Dad, Scott. I don't need to hear it from you, too."

"Oh really?" he said, "And what good has that ever done? Has it ever brought you down to a world where you're not always going to *be* the center of attention?"

He was right, of course.

"I never asked for any of this, Scott. You just have no idea." my voice was louder than my throat could stand beneath the weight of the wails of pain I was holding back.

He ignored what I said.

353

"And just when things are looking up for you! Madison was going to stay the rest of the summer, Faith. Now you'll be lucky if you don't lose one of the only people who was always on your side. Can't you imagine how she must have felt?!"

"You don't know what you're talking about!" I screamed. "You don't know anything!"

"Oh yeah?" he said, "Well then answer this for me; why didn't she come back with you?"

I said nothing. He couldn't have known. How could he have known?

"I just got off the phone with her before you walked in, Faith. She said you two argued. She wouldn't tell me what it was about, but I think it's easy enough to guess. You give her a fit for making you come home, say some things you don't mean, and expect it all to be forgiven the next day for something that happened two *years* ago."

As the last words made way from his mouth, I could tell that he already regretted them. But he was right. He spoke for all those I'd burdened with the existence I'd developed as the depression grew and took control. He spoke for the feet I'd stepped on and those who had excused my words and actions as the result of the pain I had endured. Even Todd knew that I was no good, so much so that he did not wish to make me the final love he had in this life. That's why he designated such a role for someone far more worthy than I. How could I blame Madison for being better, for being more deserving of him? I retreated up the stairs to my bedroom, fully prepared in that moment to initiate the solution to their suffering.

Letter #300

Dear Todd,

There's hope now. I can see it, Todd. I can feel it. There's so much of it, I could just scream. Madison and I went to The Pier today. Nothing seemed out of the ordinary until we were up on the Ferris Wheel, looking down at the world beneath our feet. Why couldn't I see it before? Why couldn't you and everyone like you have seen it before it was too late? There is so much hope for me, there's so much for everyone. It's so real, and it's everywhere!

~Faith

Chapter Twenty-Six

The streets of The Grove were quiet that night. The air was thick and heavy beneath the weight of all the wrongs of that little piece of world, all the things that went unnoticed or ignored.

Madison Baker sat in the driver's seat of her mother's convertible in their driveway, listening to the waves across the street through the open window. Her fingers rested on the keys, which sat still in the car's ignition as they had for the past fifteen minutes.

Faith Anderson sat, too. But she was not in

the passenger's seat of Madison's mother's convertible. She was instead on the floor of her closet, running her fingers over the rope she retrieved from her father's shed after her brother, Scott, went to bed.

The world sat still.

Madison watched a lady bug climb across the windshield toward her right side-view mirror. The passing breeze occasionally delayed its journey, and she was tempted for a moment to get out of the car, pick it up, and set it down in the place where it was headed. But she did not know where that was. And doing so would mean getting out of the car, thus halting her own journey. So she watched until the bug opened its wings, leapt off the side of the car, and soared in the direction of its own pursuit, deciding then that it was about time she do the same.

Faith watched the clock, wondering how long it would be before her parents went to bed. They had already come upstairs and said goodnight, but from the crack beneath her door she could see that the light in the hall outside her room had yet to be turned off, as was a common procedure in bedtime ritual in the Anderson household.

The car moved much faster than Madison

had initially intended, but she didn't mind. She watched the speedometer religiously, going into momentary panic any time it exceeded fifteen miles per hour. She remembered that day in upstate New York when she'd gone to visit her grandparents' estate. It was a few days after her seventeenth birthday. A few months since she had left The Grove. A few hours since she'd said goodbye to her father and boarded the train up to her grandparents' estate. She remembered the brand new, cherry red car her grandfather drove out when she arrived. The brand new, cherry red car that was given to her as a birthday present. The brand new, cherry red car that she took out and drove for miles until she came

across a tree. She remembered that the leaves on the

tree were changing and how, God, were they

beautiful. She remembered sobbing on the phone

with her grandparents, telling them she was being

foolish, she was driving too fast. She remembered

her grandmother telling her that everyone makes

mistakes, that it was fine and her father didn't need

to know. She remembered the moment she decided

to plow into that great, big, beautiful tree, and she

remembered the moment she turned the wheel at the

very last second. That last second, when she

regretted what had yet to be done and decided to

change it. That last second that we all hope people like her can get. She remembered these things, but she kept driving.

Faith decided to ignore the light beneath her door. They had probably just forgotten.

Madison came to a fork in the road. On one side was Fraigle Street, down which was Faith Anderson's home. On the other side, Ocean Avenue continued off into the horizon. She stopped the car and put it in park, right there in the middle of the road. She glanced at her phone, which rested alone on her passenger's seat.

Faith held the rope around her neck and

began to stand, then hesitated, looking down at the floor, where her cell phone resided. It was on, of course, as she had been frequently checking the time. She stood up and looked back down at the phone, watching it.

Madison kept her eyes steady on her phone. She wondered how Faith was doing. She wondered if it was even worth calling, since Faith must have hated her by that point. She probably wouldn't even pick up. It was two o'clock in the morning.

Faith watched the phone and remained still with the rope around her neck. She was afraid, so she waited. For what, she didn't know. But she waited. She waited and watched the phone on the floor.

Madison made her decision and slid the key back into the ignition. But before she could pursue it, her eyes wandered back to the phone on her seat.

Faith drew in a breath, her eyes on the phone.

Everything stopped. Everything stopped just long enough for all that was and had been and could be to be recognized and taken into account before the world went back to turning.

Have Hope.

Keep Faith.

The End.

Letter #1

Dear Reader,

Don't let it end here. Whether or not faith dies is your choice, not mine. Please don't hate me for this. Thank you for reading. I love you.

Shannon Schmidt.

www.ingramcontent.com/pod-product-compliance
Lightning Source LLC
Chambersburg PA
CBHW070759180626
46818CB00001B/24